STAR WARS™
RETURN OF THE JEDI

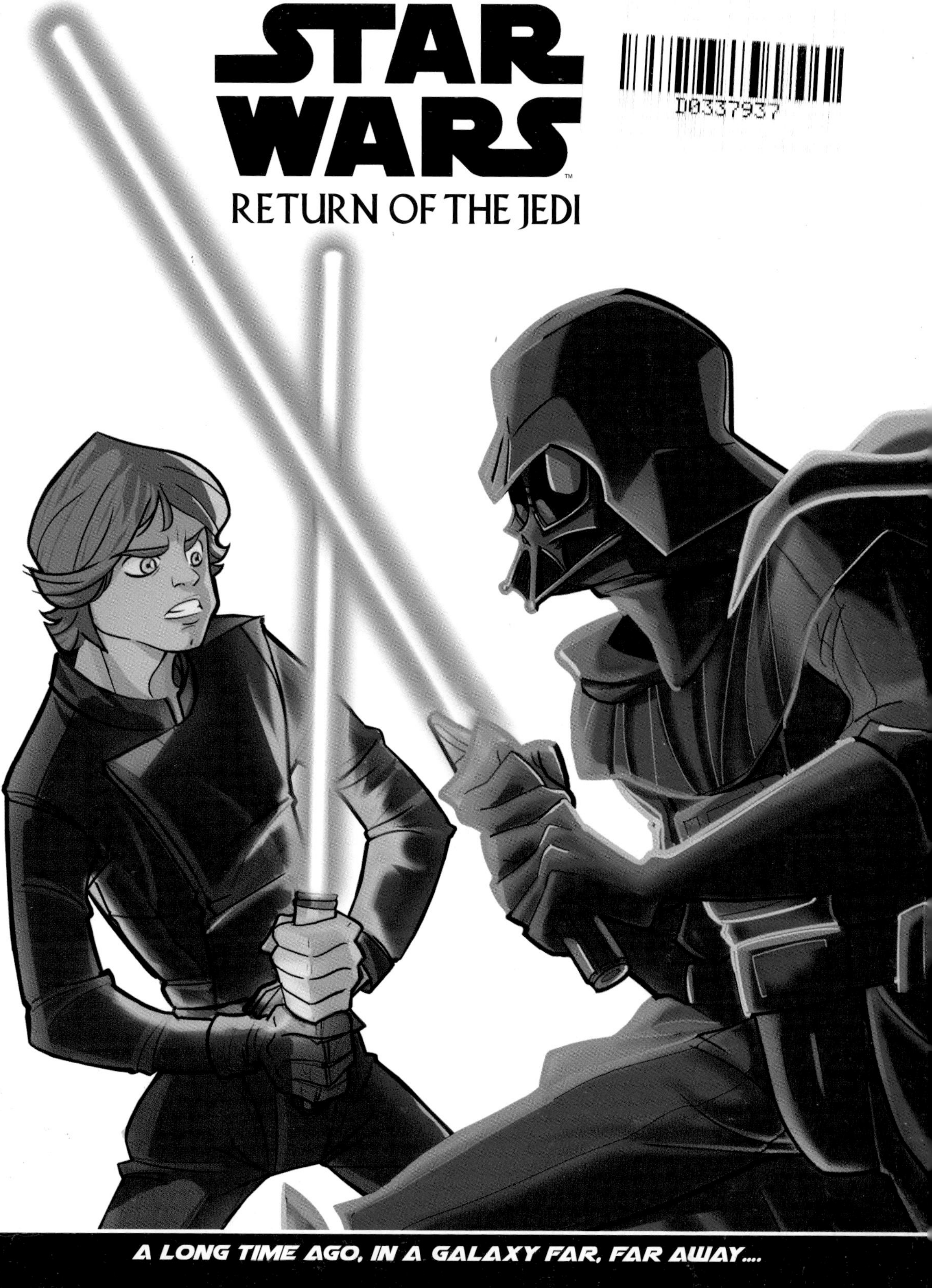

A LONG TIME AGO, IN A GALAXY FAR, FAR AWAY....

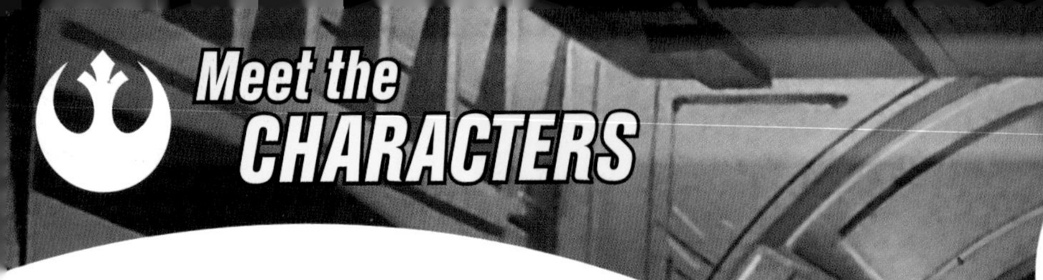

Meet the CHARACTERS

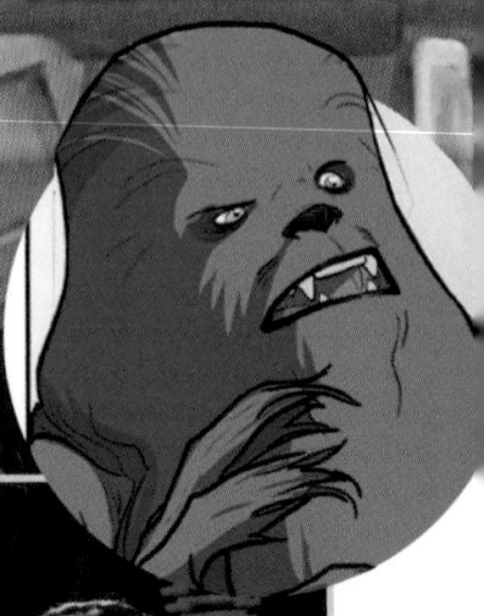

LUKE SKYWALKER

Luke's training is not complete yet. In order to become a **Jedi**, he must confront his worst fear: **his father**, the Sith Lord Darth Vader. But right now Luke is far away, on his home planet **Tatooine**: he has built a new **lightsaber** and prepares to rescue his friend **Han Solo** from **Jabba the Hutt's palace**.

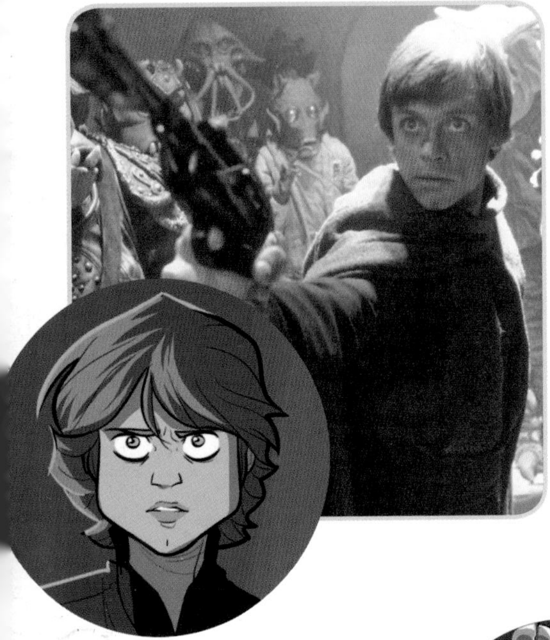

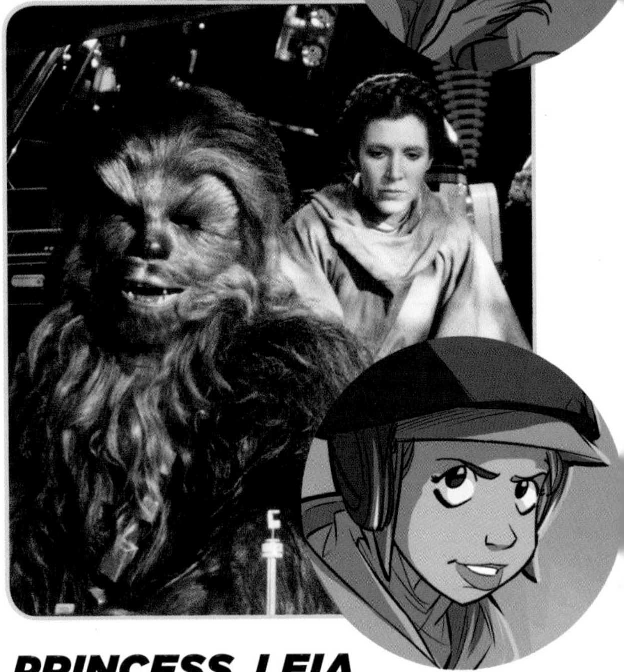

PRINCESS LEIA ORGANA & CHEWBACCA

Following Luke's plan, Leia reached Tatooine too, together with **Han's first mate** and **friend**, the Wookiee Chewbacca. Leia would do anything to save the man she loves from a horrible destiny.

C-3PO & R2-D2

C-3PO and his counterpart, the astromech droid R2-D2, are also part of **Luke's plan**; however only R2-D2 is aware of how **dangerous** and **risky** that plan is going to be.

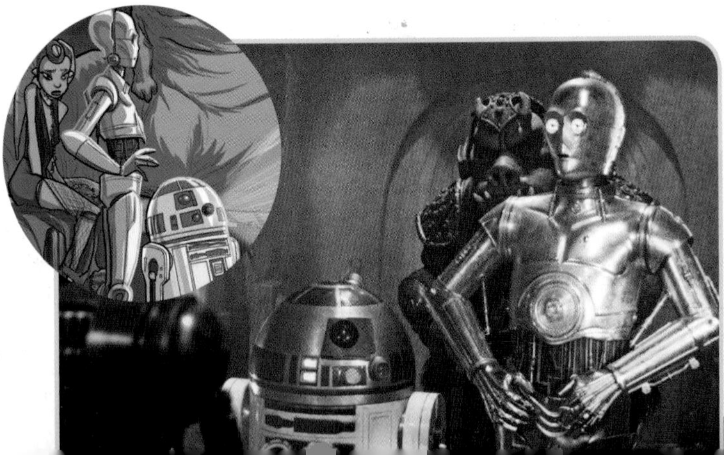

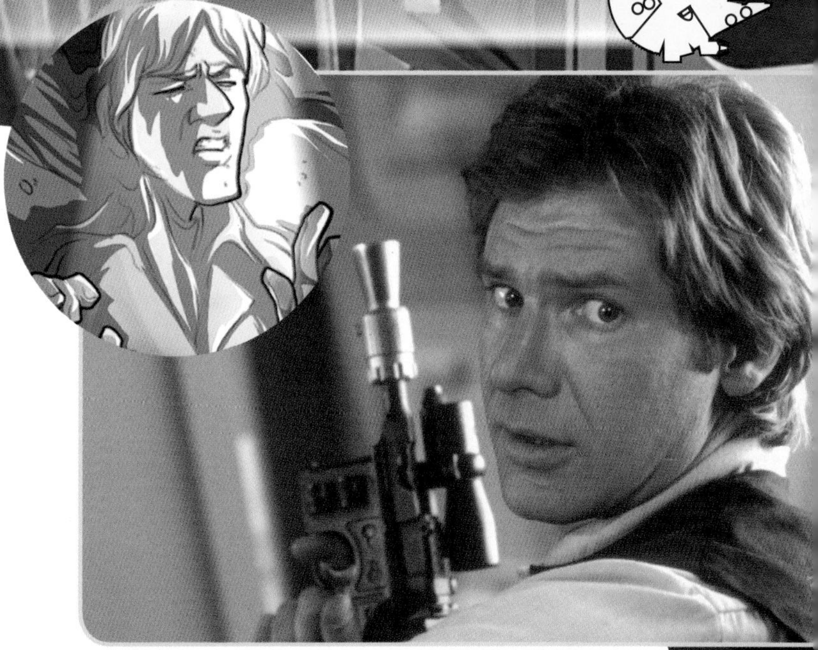

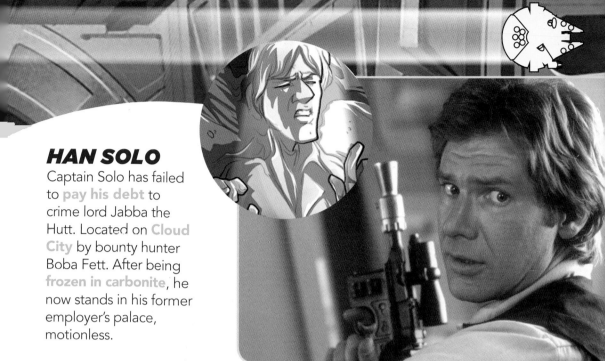

HAN SOLO

Captain Solo has failed to **pay his debt** to crime lord Jabba the Hutt. Located on **Cloud City** by bounty hunter Boba Fett. After being **frozen in carbonite**, he now stands in his former employer's palace, motionless.

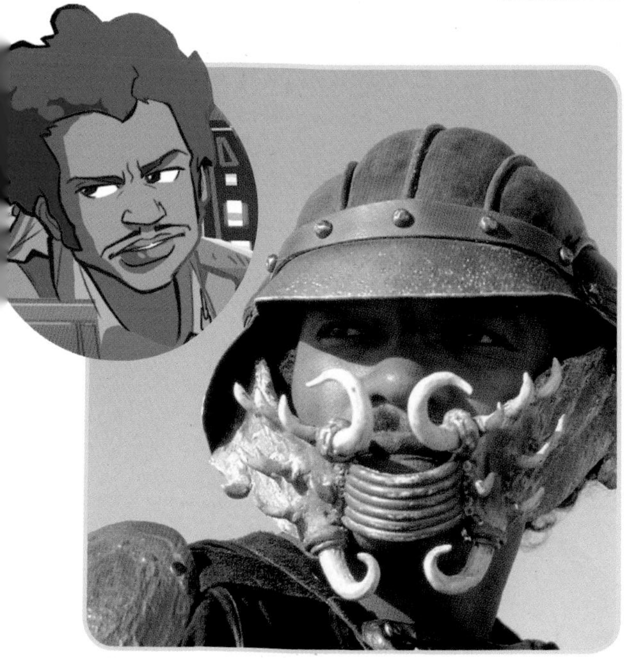

EWOKS

These **small**, **furry creatures** live in harmony with the natural world around them: the **primeval woods** of the **Forest Moon of Endor**. Curious and peaceful, their thorough knowledge of the forest makes them a very useful ally in the battle against the heavily equipped Imperial stormtroopers.

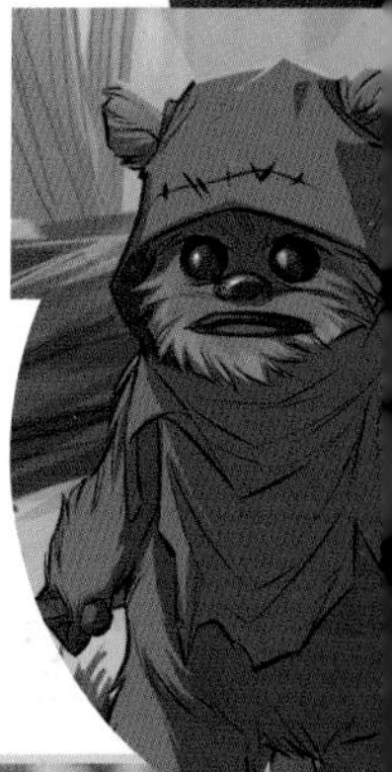

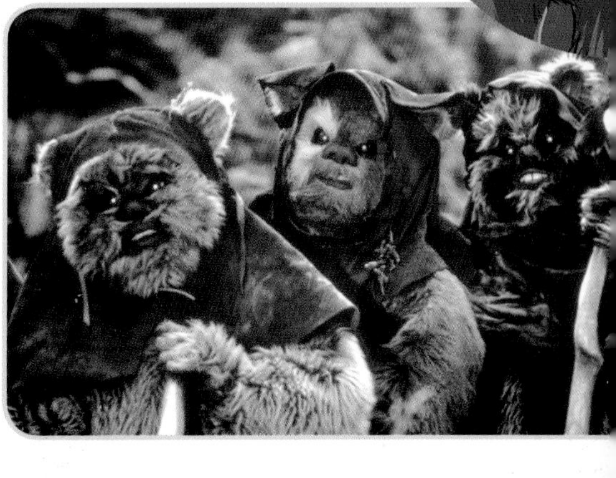

LANDO CALRISSIAN

Even though he betrayed his old friend Han Solo, Lando redeemed himself by **saving Leia and Chewbacca** from the Imperial troops. He now fights for the **Rebellion** and waits for Skywalker in Jabba's palace, disguised as one of the gangster's guards.

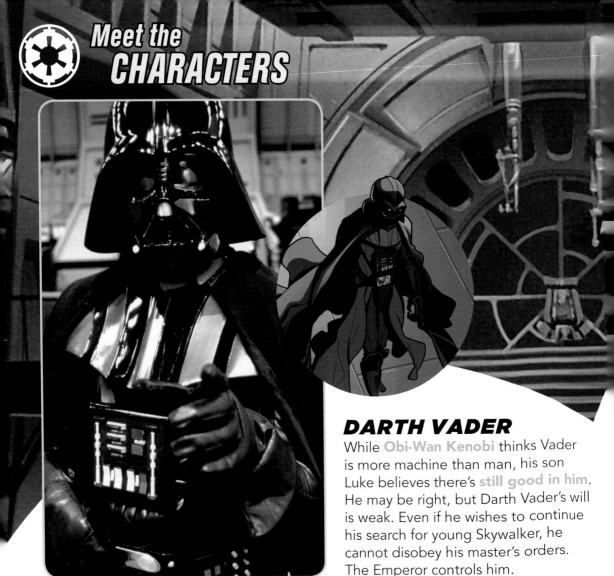

DARTH VADER

While **Obi-Wan Kenobi** thinks Vader is more machine than man, his son Luke believes there's **still good in him**. He may be right, but Darth Vader's will is weak. Even if he wishes to continue his search for young Skywalker, he cannot disobey his master's orders. The Emperor controls him.

JABBA THE HUTT

Hutts run many of the galaxy's large criminal syndicates. **Jabba Desilijic Tiure**, known as Jabba the Hutt, comes from the planet **Nal Hutta**, where he was raised to crave power and wealth. Equipped with a cunning criminal mind, Jabba is highly intelligent, and rarely overlooks details or dangers.

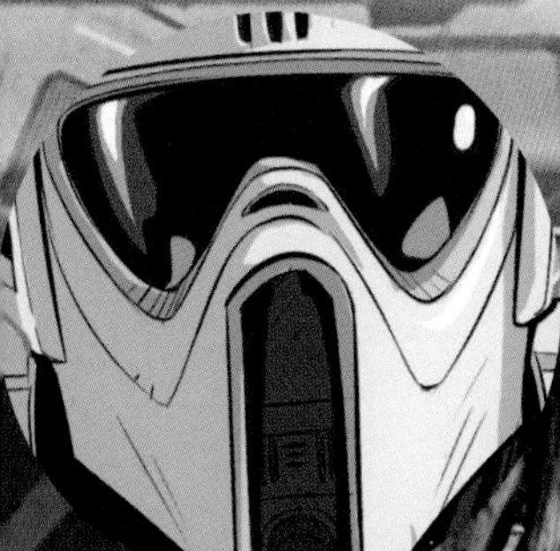

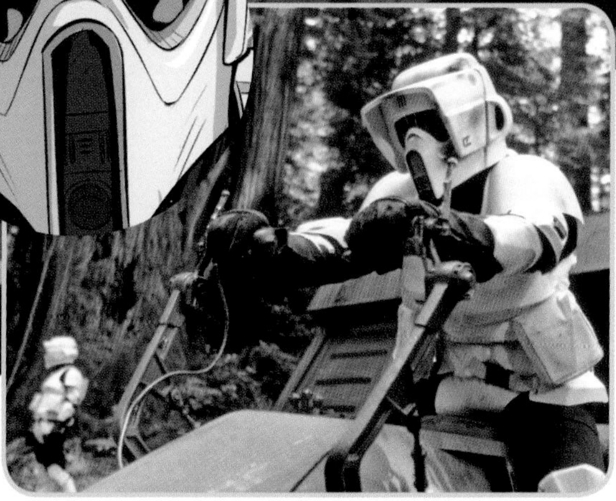

BIKER SCOUTS

Biker scouts are equipped for high maneuverability and long periods without support. They patrol the **Forest Moon of Endor**, constantly on the lookout for rebels, riding exceptionally fast Aratech 74-Z **speeder bikes**.

BIB FORTUNA

As the **chief lieutenant**, Bib Fortuna supervises the **affairs of Jabba's desert palace**. His control within the organization and his tendency to resort to underhanded means with friends and foes alike make him a **powerful** and **dreaded**, if **cowardly**, individual.

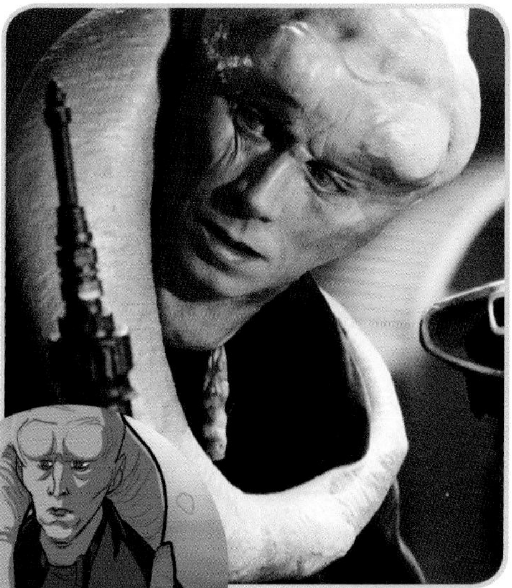

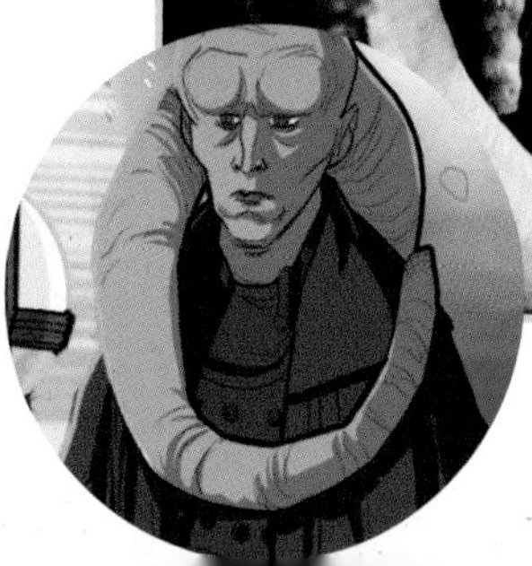

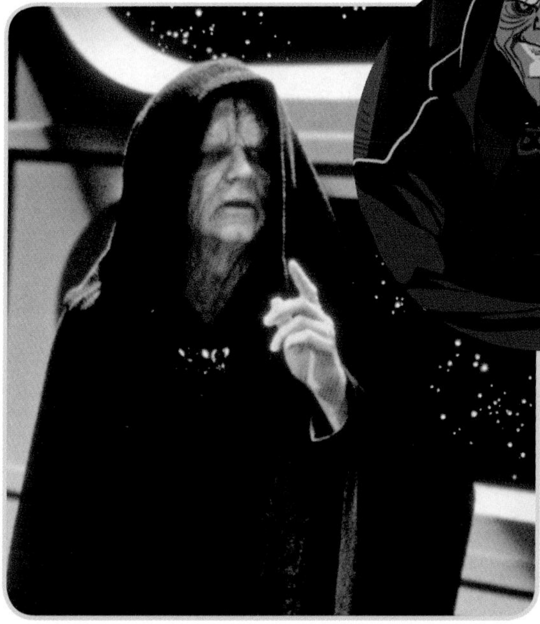

EMPEROR PALPATINE

Once **Supreme Chancellor** of the **Republic**, Palpatine is now the **supreme ruler** of the **Empire**. Evil and manipulative, he is ready to destroy all who challenge him. The Emperor is one of the most powerful Sith Lords who ever lived: the dark side of the Force gives him incredible powers and has sustained him beyond his years.

Episode VI
RETURN OF THE JEDI

Luke Skywalker has returned to
his home planet of Tatooine in
an attempt to rescue his
friend Han Solo from the
clutches of the vile gangster
Jabba the Hutt.

Little does Luke know that the
GALACTIC EMPIRE has secretly
begun construction on a new
armored space station even
more powerful than the first
dreaded Death Star.

When completed, this ultimate
weapon will spell certain doom
for the small band of rebels
struggling to restore freedom
to the galaxy.....

FOREST MOON OF ENDOR. THE NEW DEATH STAR.

COMMAND STATION, THIS IS ST 321. CODE CLEARANCE BLUE.

WE'RE STARTING OUR APPROACH. DEACTIVATE THE SECURITY SHIELD.

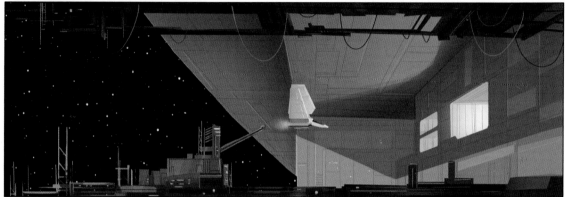

LORD VADER, THIS IS AN UNEXPECTED PLEASURE. WE'RE HONORED BY YOUR PRESENCE.

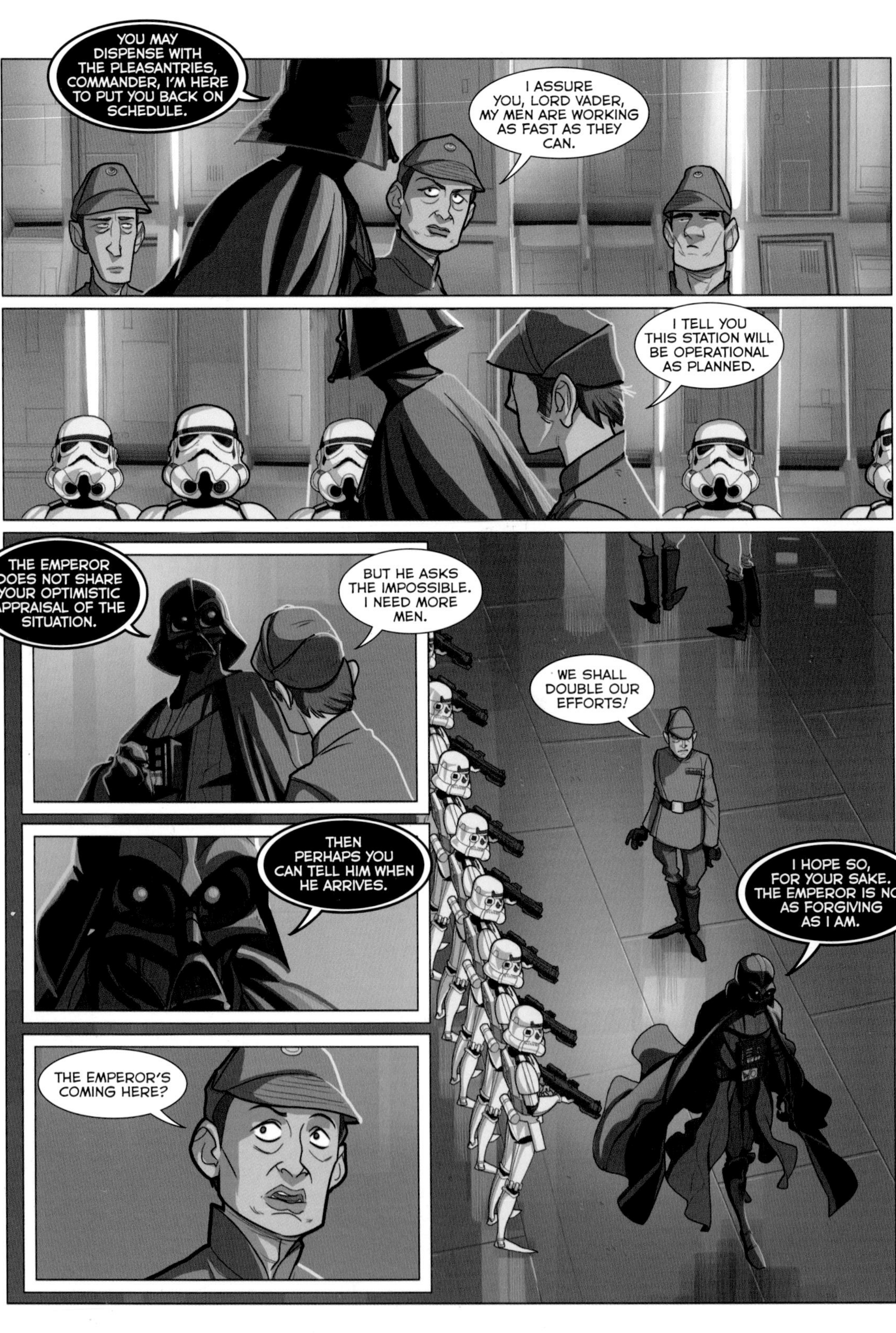
YOU MAY DISPENSE WITH THE PLEASANTRIES, COMMANDER, I'M HERE TO PUT YOU BACK ON SCHEDULE.
I ASSURE YOU, LORD VADER, MY MEN ARE WORKING AS FAST AS THEY CAN.
I TELL YOU THIS STATION WILL BE OPERATIONAL AS PLANNED.
THE EMPEROR DOES NOT SHARE YOUR OPTIMISTIC APPRAISAL OF THE SITUATION.
BUT HE ASKS THE IMPOSSIBLE. I NEED MORE MEN.
THEN PERHAPS YOU CAN TELL HIM WHEN HE ARRIVES.
THE EMPEROR'S COMING HERE?
WE SHALL DOUBLE OUR EFFORTS!
I HOPE SO, FOR YOUR SAKE. THE EMPEROR IS NOT AS FORGIVING AS I AM.

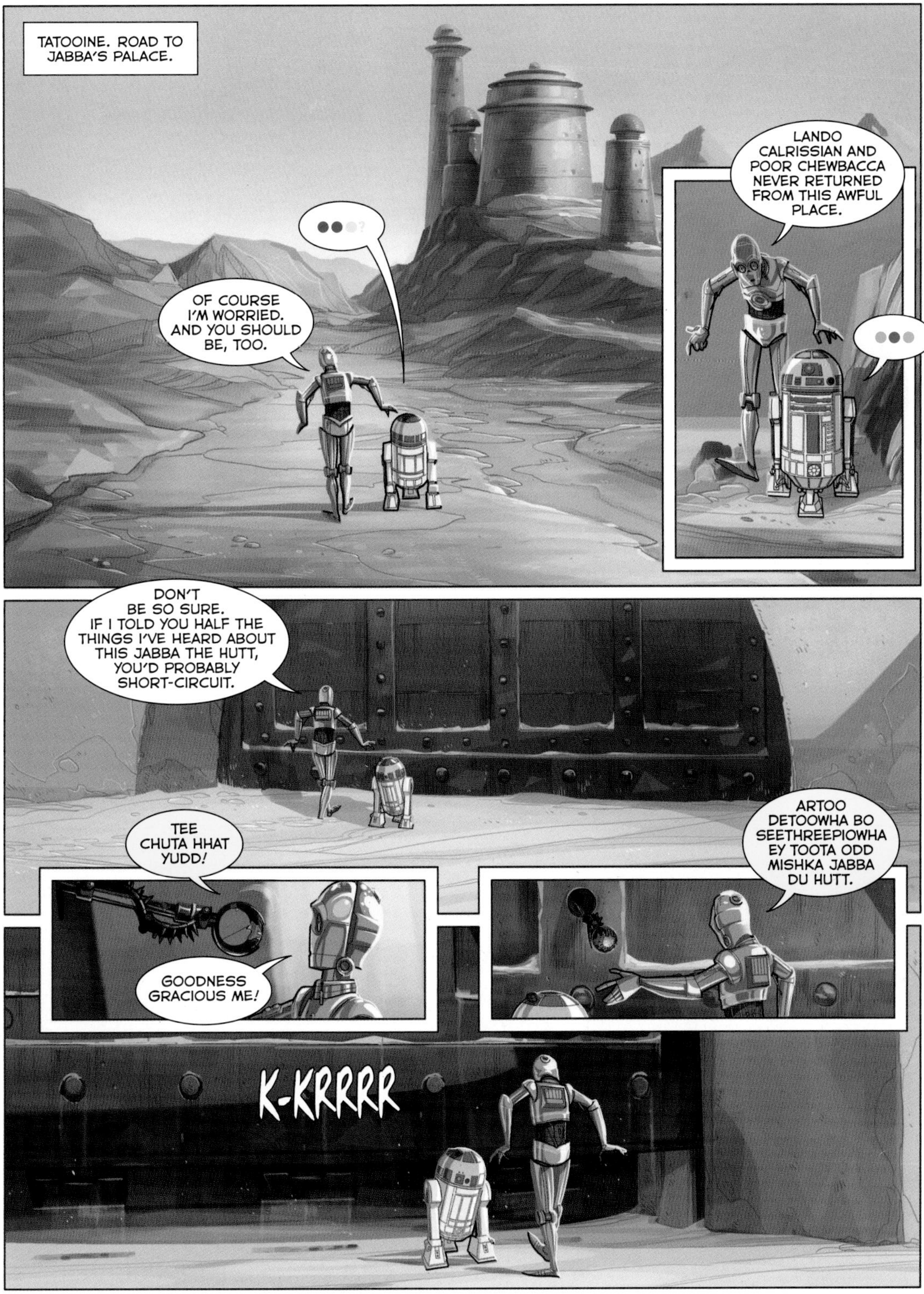
TATOOINE. ROAD TO JABBA'S PALACE.
OF COURSE I'M WORRIED. AND YOU SHOULD BE, TOO.
LANDO CALRISSIAN AND POOR CHEWBACCA NEVER RETURNED FROM THIS AWFUL PLACE.
DON'T BE SO SURE. IF I TOLD YOU HALF THE THINGS I'VE HEARD ABOUT THIS JABBA THE HUTT, YOU'D PROBABLY SHORT-CIRCUIT.
TEE CHUTA HHAT YUDD!
GOODNESS GRACIOUS ME!
ARTOO DETOOWHA BO SEETHREEPIOWHA EY TOOTA ODD MISHKA JABBA DU HUTT.
K-KRRRR

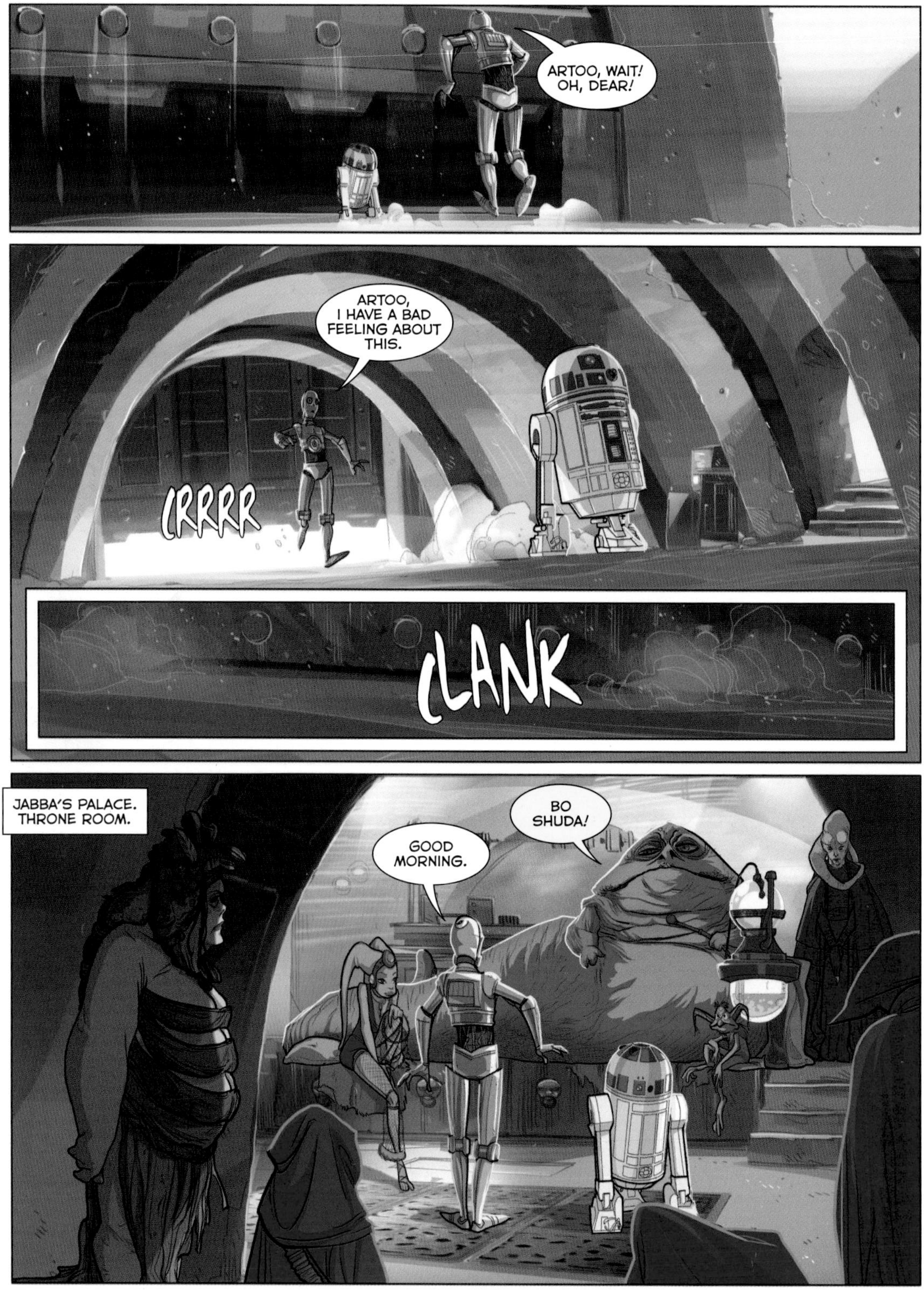
ARTOO, WAIT! OH, DEAR!
ARTOO, I HAVE A BAD FEELING ABOUT THIS.
CRRRR
CLANK
JABBA'S PALACE. THRONE ROOM.
BO SHUDA!
GOOD MORNING.

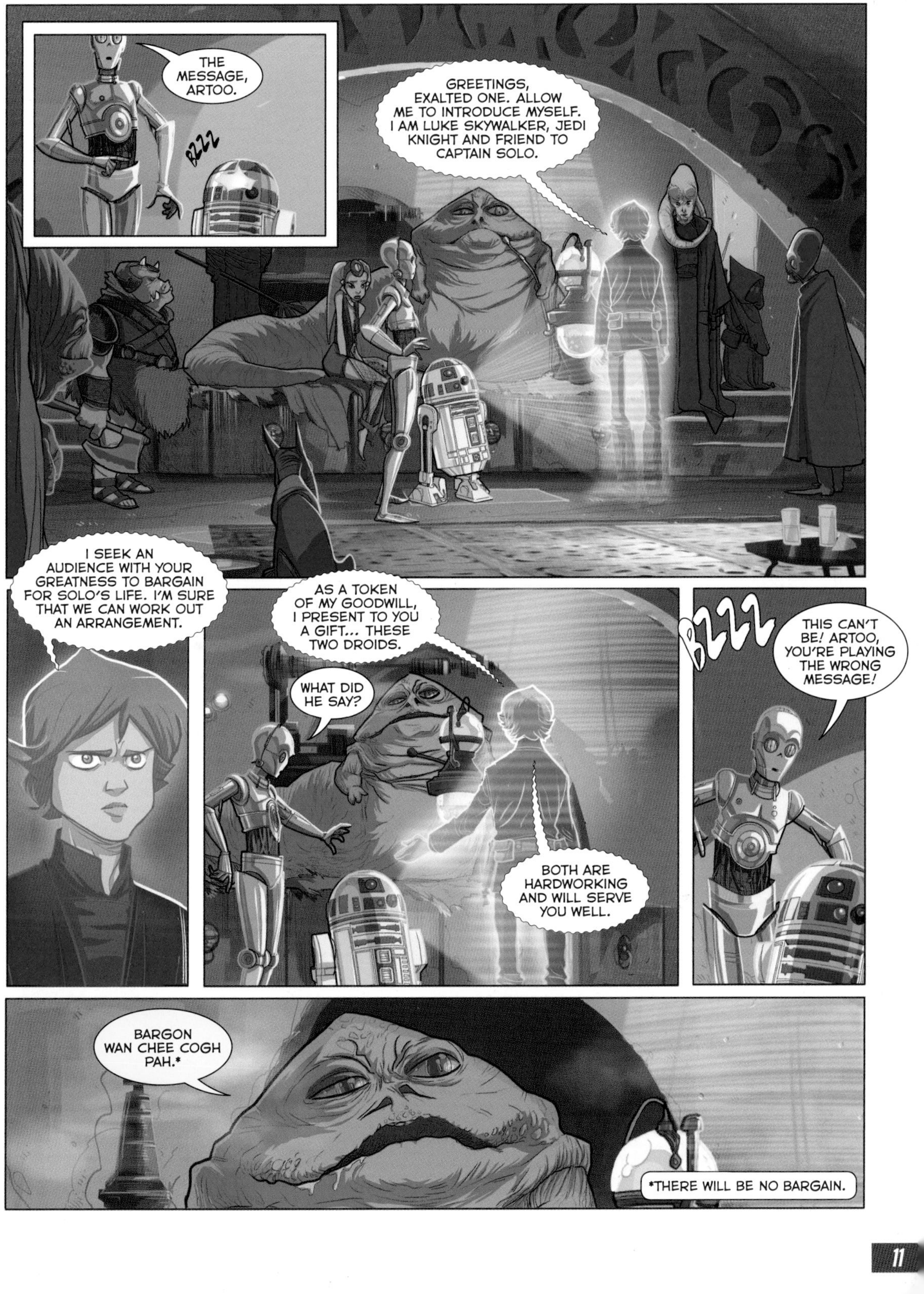
THE MESSAGE, ARTOO.
BZZZ
GREETINGS, EXALTED ONE. ALLOW ME TO INTRODUCE MYSELF. I AM LUKE SKYWALKER, JEDI KNIGHT AND FRIEND TO CAPTAIN SOLO.
I SEEK AN AUDIENCE WITH YOUR GREATNESS TO BARGAIN FOR SOLO'S LIFE. I'M SURE THAT WE CAN WORK OUT AN ARRANGEMENT.
AS A TOKEN OF MY GOODWILL, I PRESENT TO YOU A GIFT... THESE TWO DROIDS.
WHAT DID HE SAY?
BOTH ARE HARDWORKING AND WILL SERVE YOU WELL.
BZZZ
THIS CAN'T BE! ARTOO, YOU'RE PLAYING THE WRONG MESSAGE!
BARGON WAN CHEE COGH PAH.*
*THERE WILL BE NO BARGAIN.

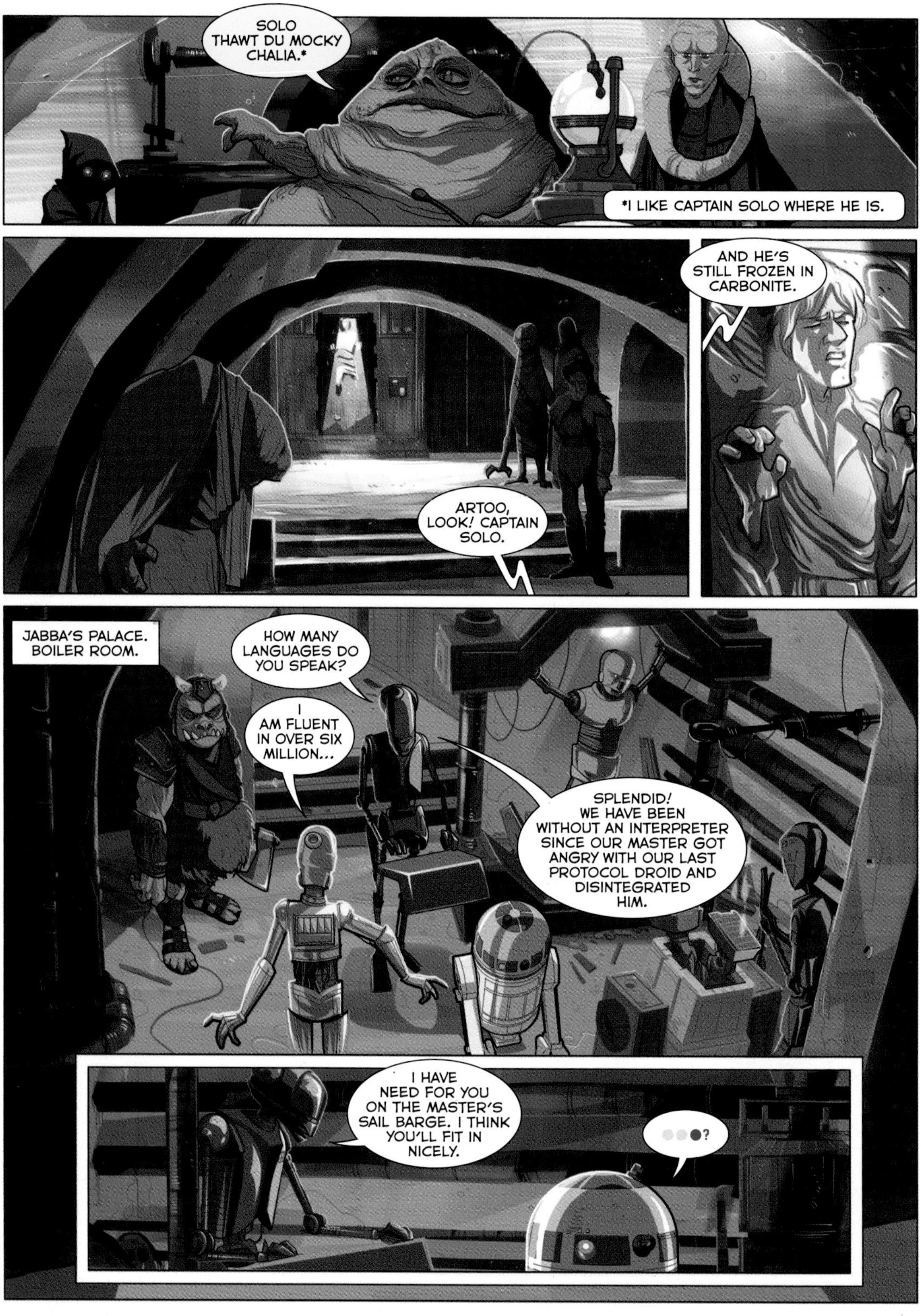
SOLO THAWT DU MOCKY CHALIA.*
*I LIKE CAPTAIN SOLO WHERE HE IS.
ARTOO, LOOK! CAPTAIN SOLO.
AND HE'S STILL FROZEN IN CARBONITE.
JABBA'S PALACE. BOILER ROOM.
HOW MANY LANGUAGES DO YOU SPEAK?
I AM FLUENT IN OVER SIX MILLION...
SPLENDID! WE HAVE BEEN WITHOUT AN INTERPRETER SINCE OUR MASTER GOT ANGRY WITH OUR LAST PROTOCOL DROID AND DISINTEGRATED HIM.
I HAVE NEED FOR YOU ON THE MASTER'S SAIL BARGE. I THINK YOU'LL FIT IN NICELY.
?

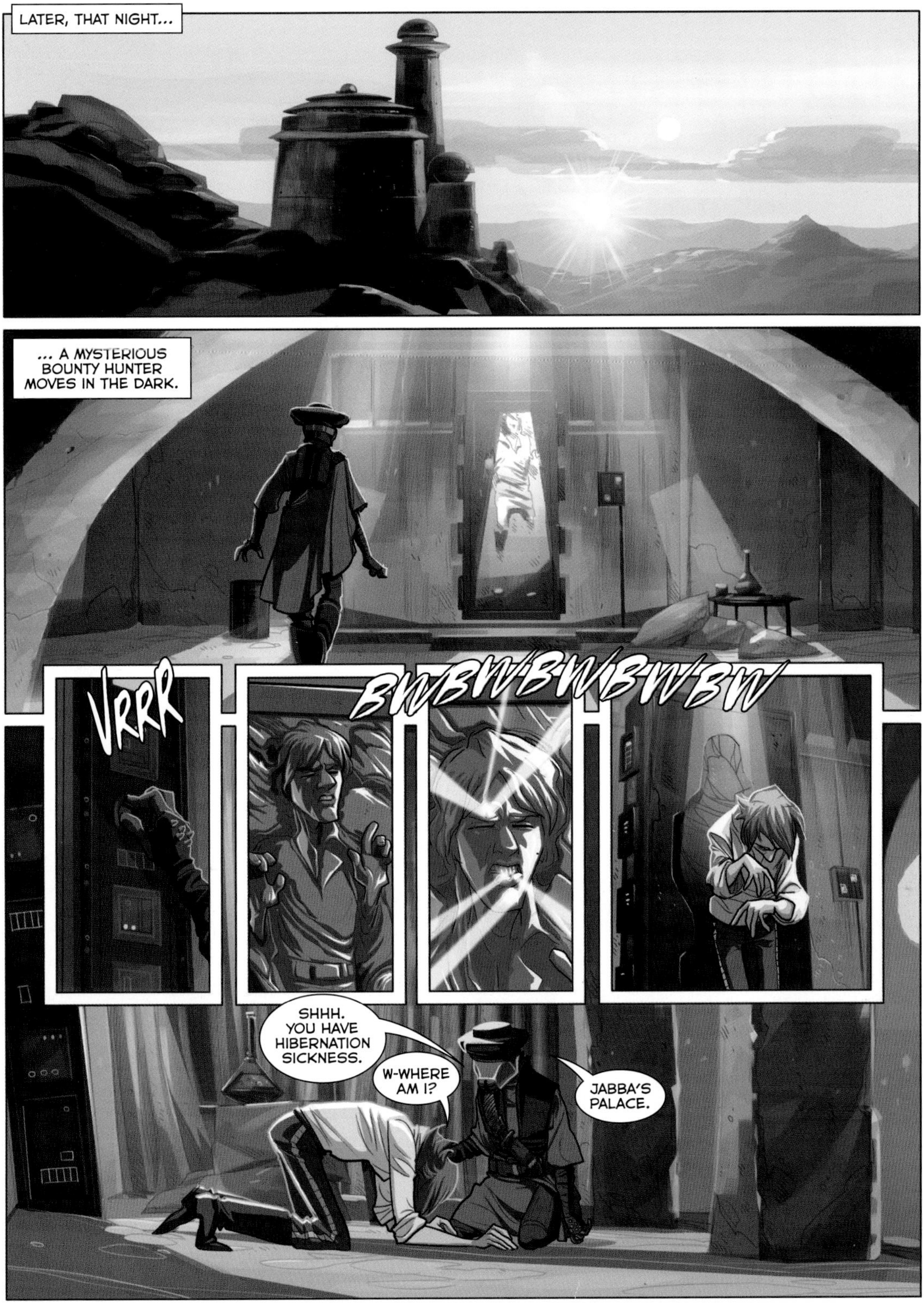
LATER, THAT NIGHT...
... A MYSTERIOUS BOUNTY HUNTER MOVES IN THE DARK.
VRRR
BWBWBWBWBW
SHHH. YOU HAVE HIBERNATION SICKNESS.
W-WHERE AM I?
JABBA'S PALACE.

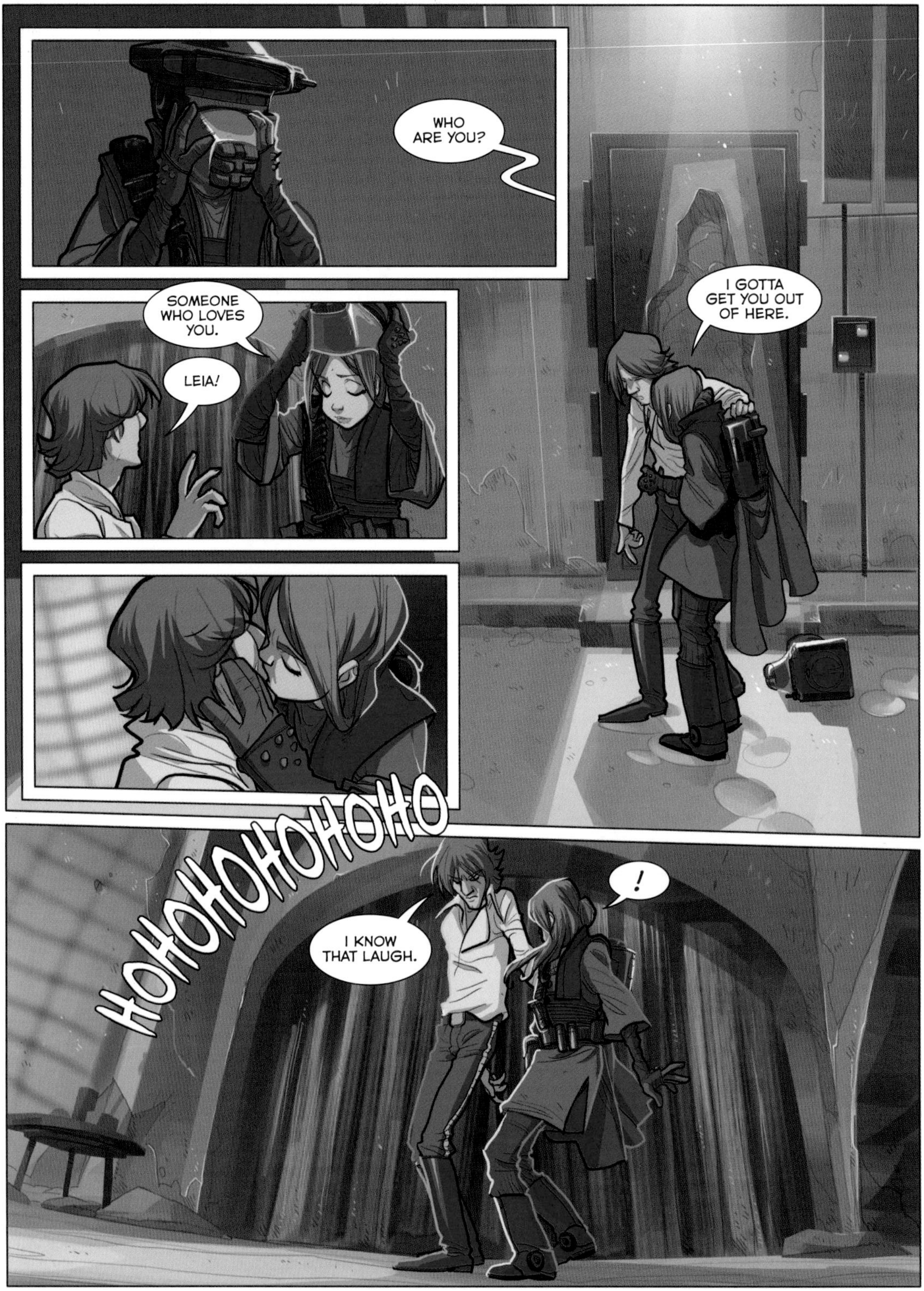

WHO ARE YOU?
SOMEONE WHO LOVES YOU.
LEIA!
I GOTTA GET YOU OUT OF HERE.
HOHOHOHOHOHOHOHO
I KNOW THAT LAUGH.
!

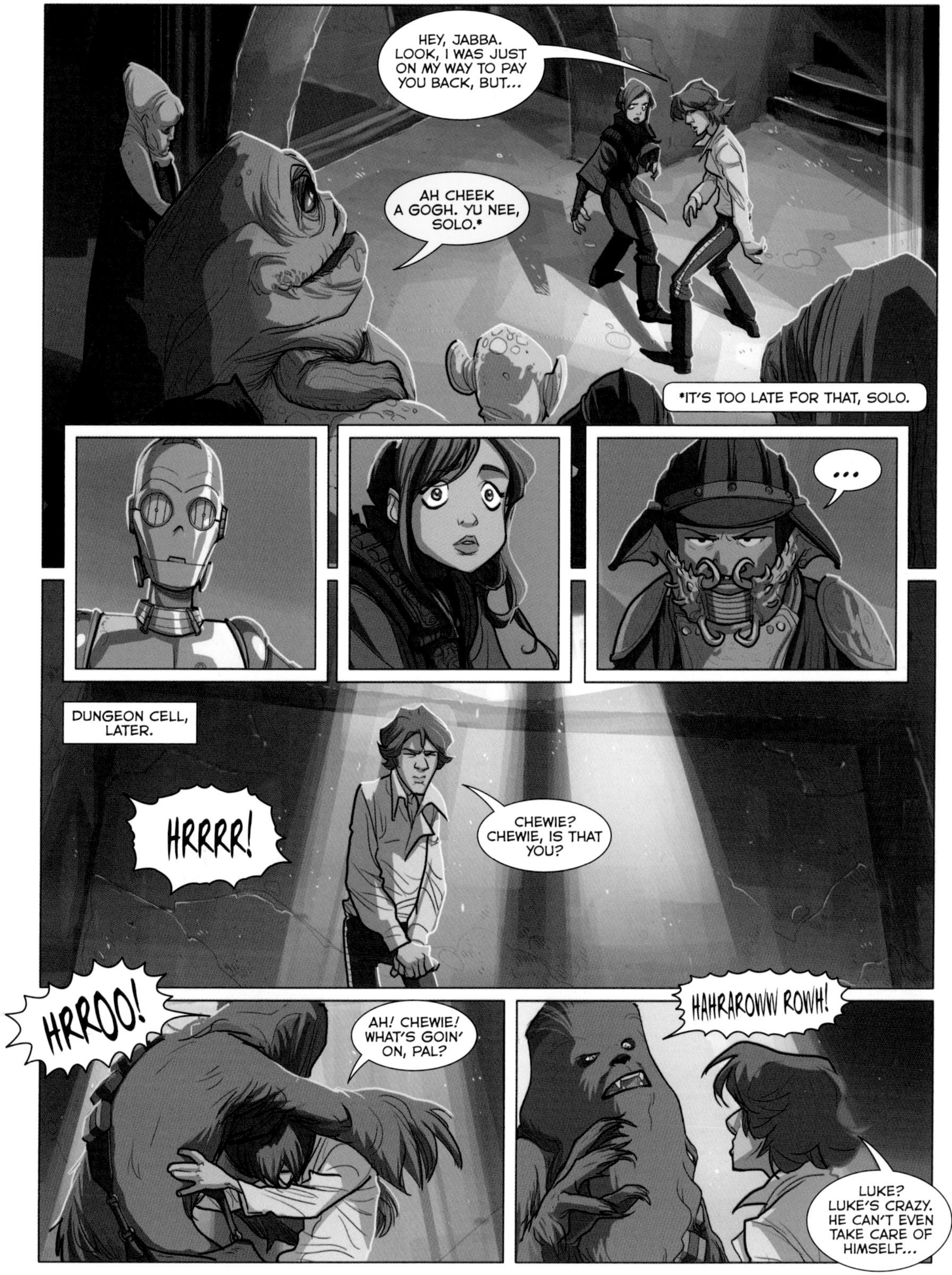
HEY, JABBA. LOOK, I WAS JUST ON MY WAY TO PAY YOU BACK, BUT...
AH CHEEK A GOGH. YU NEE, SOLO.*
*IT'S TOO LATE FOR THAT, SOLO.
...
DUNGEON CELL, LATER.
HRRRR!
CHEWIE? CHEWIE, IS THAT YOU?
HRROO!
AH! CHEWIE! WHAT'S GOIN' ON, PAL?
HAHRAROWW ROWH!
LUKE? LUKE'S CRAZY. HE CAN'T EVEN TAKE CARE OF HIMSELF...

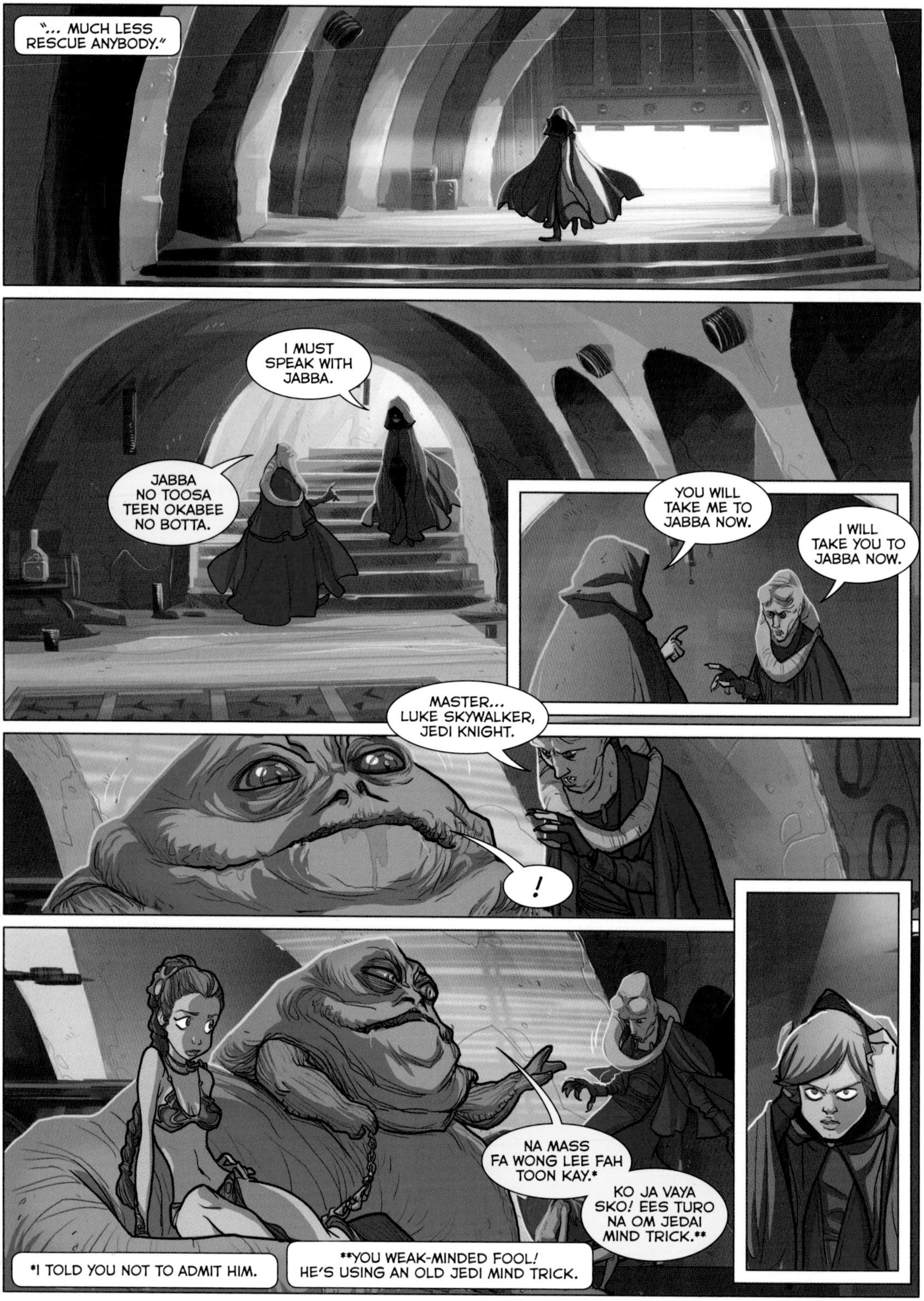
"... MUCH LESS RESCUE ANYBODY."
I MUST SPEAK WITH JABBA.
JABBA NO TOOSA TEEN OKABEE NO BOTTA.
YOU WILL TAKE ME TO JABBA NOW.
I WILL TAKE YOU TO JABBA NOW.
MASTER... LUKE SKYWALKER, JEDI KNIGHT.
!
NA MASS FA WONG LEE FAH TOON KAY.*
KO JA VAYA SKO! EES TURO NA OM JEDAI MIND TRICK.**
*I TOLD YOU NOT TO ADMIT HIM.
**YOU WEAK-MINDED FOOL! HE'S USING AN OLD JEDI MIND TRICK.

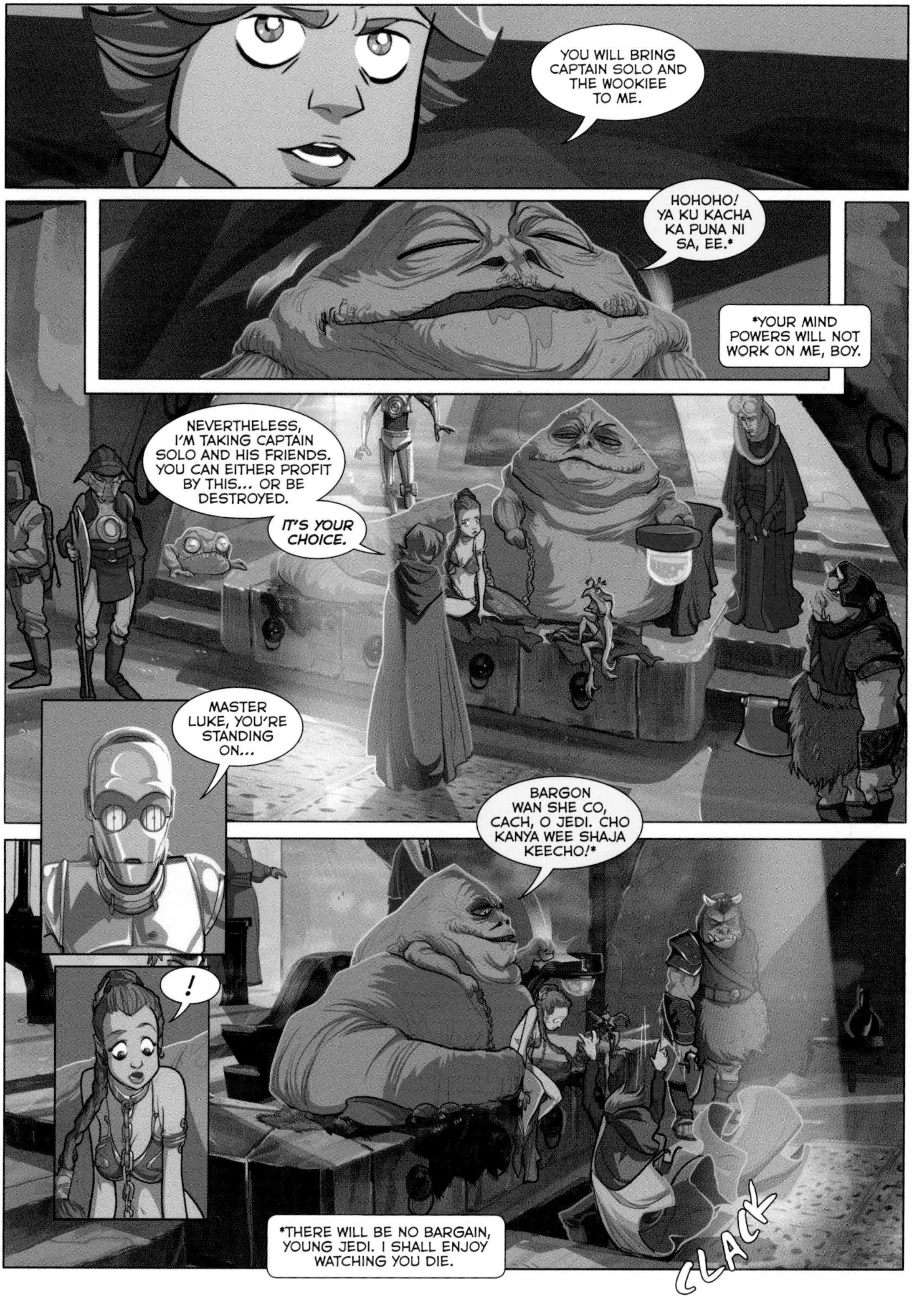
YOU WILL BRING CAPTAIN SOLO AND THE WOOKIEE TO ME.
HOHOHO! YA KU KACHA KA PUNA NI SA, EE.*
*YOUR MIND POWERS WILL NOT WORK ON ME, BOY.
NEVERTHELESS, I'M TAKING CAPTAIN SOLO AND HIS FRIENDS. YOU CAN EITHER PROFIT BY THIS... OR BE DESTROYED.
IT'S YOUR CHOICE.
MASTER LUKE, YOU'RE STANDING ON...
BARGON WAN SHE CO, CACH, O JEDI. CHO KANYA WEE SHAJA KEECHO!*
!
*THERE WILL BE NO BARGAIN, YOUNG JEDI. I SHALL ENJOY WATCHING YOU DIE.
CLACK

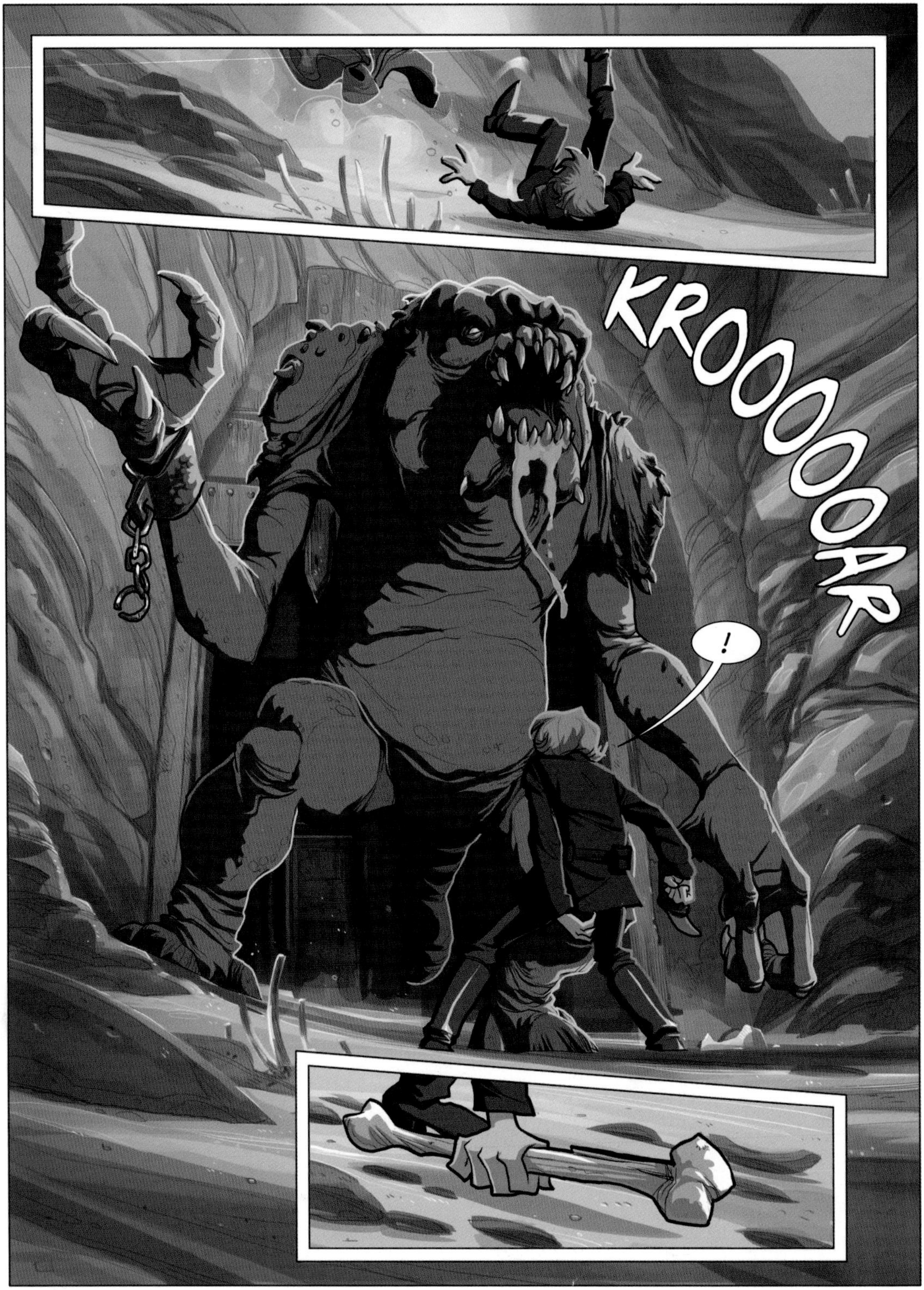
KROOOOOAR
!

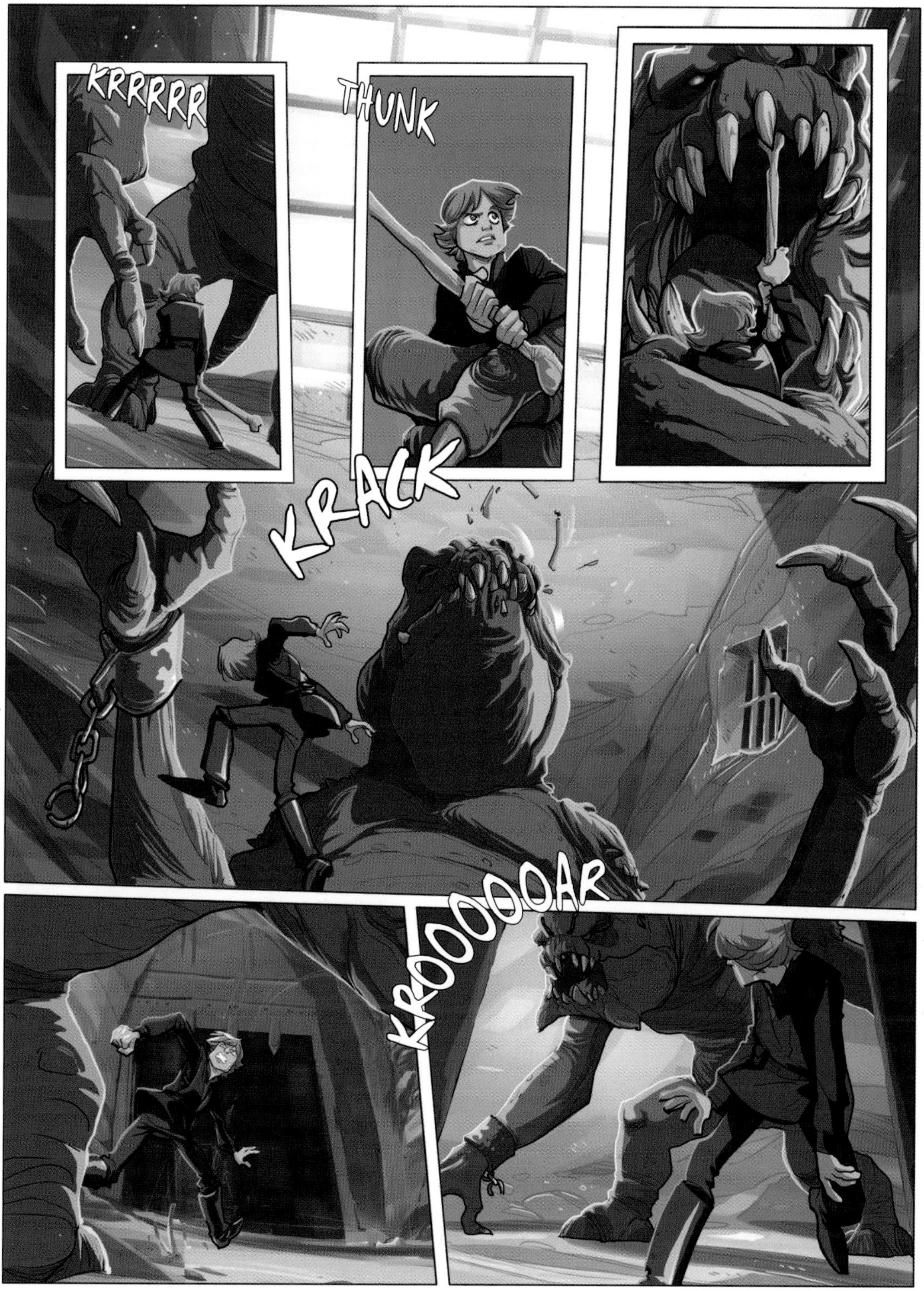
KRRRRR
THUNK
KRACK
KROOOOOAR

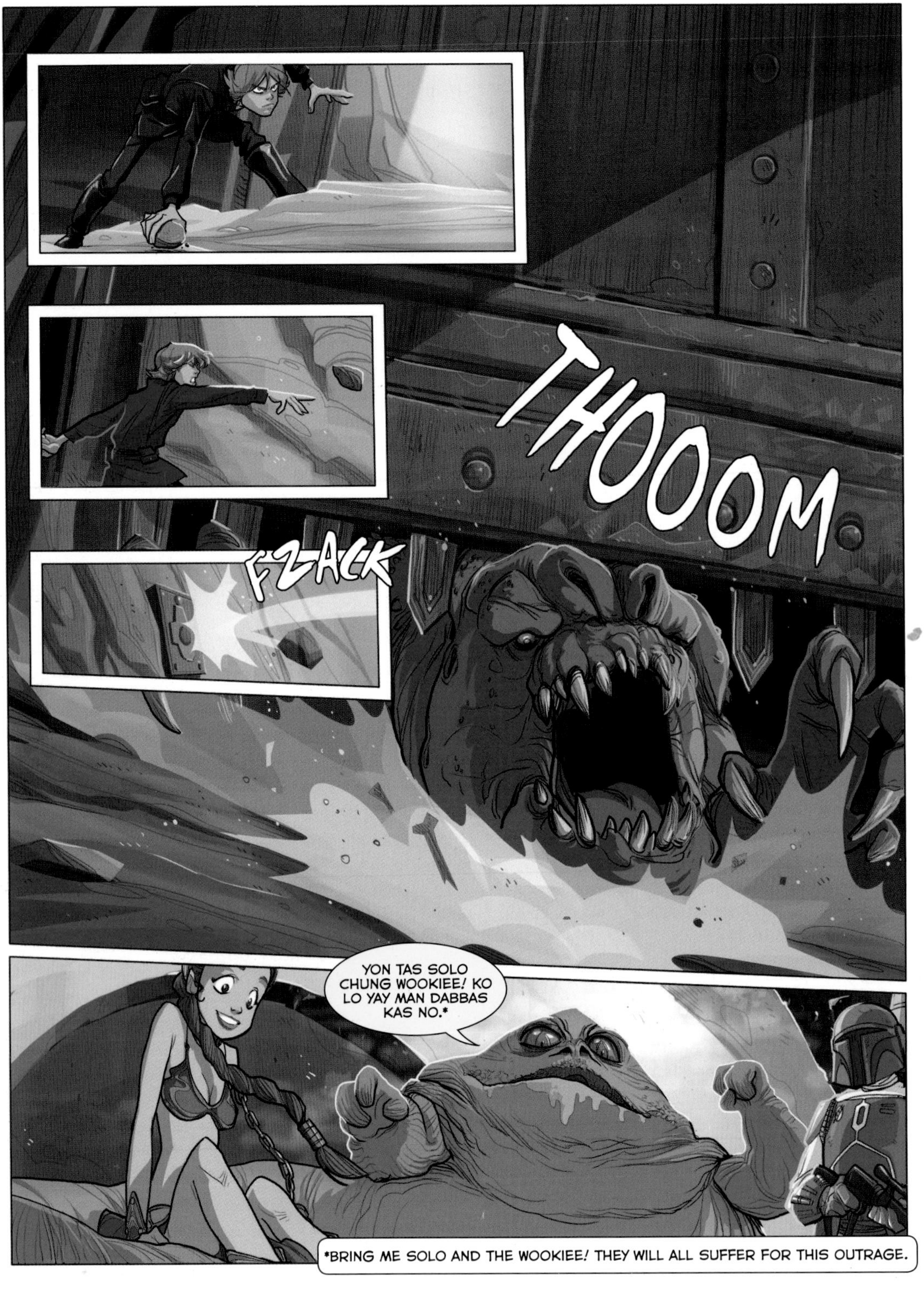

THOOOM
FZACK
YON TAS SOLO CHUNG WOOKIEE! KO LO YAY MAN DABBAS KAS NO.*
*BRING ME SOLO AND THE WOOKIEE! THEY WILL ALL SUFFER FOR THIS OUTRAGE.

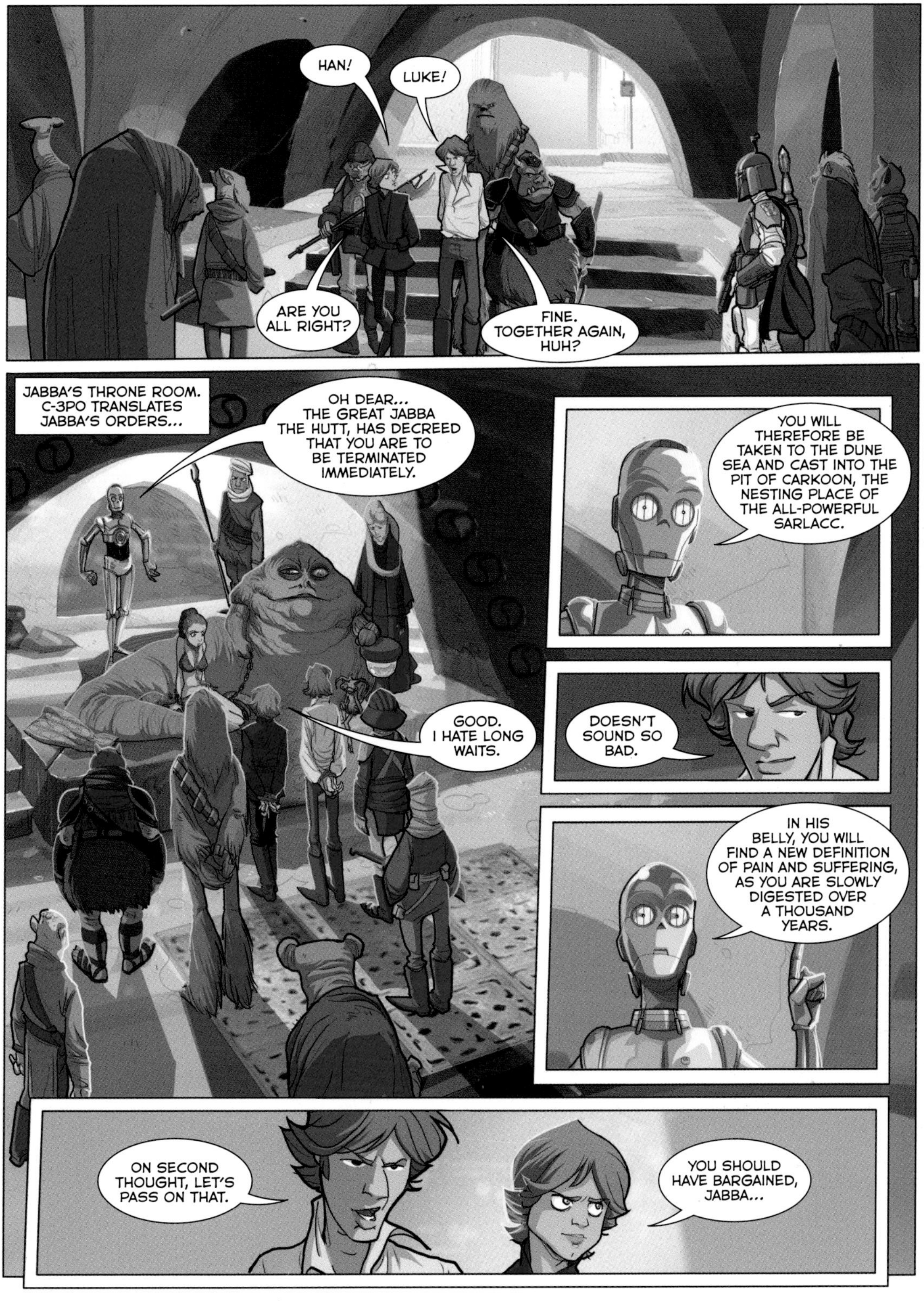
HAN!
LUKE!
ARE YOU ALL RIGHT?
FINE. TOGETHER AGAIN, HUH?
JABBA'S THRONE ROOM. C-3PO TRANSLATES JABBA'S ORDERS...
OH DEAR... THE GREAT JABBA THE HUTT, HAS DECREED THAT YOU ARE TO BE TERMINATED IMMEDIATELY.
GOOD. I HATE LONG WAITS.
YOU WILL THEREFORE BE TAKEN TO THE DUNE SEA AND CAST INTO THE PIT OF CARKOON, THE NESTING PLACE OF THE ALL-POWERFUL SARLACC.
DOESN'T SOUND SO BAD.
IN HIS BELLY, YOU WILL FIND A NEW DEFINITION OF PAIN AND SUFFERING, AS YOU ARE SLOWLY DIGESTED OVER A THOUSAND YEARS.
ON SECOND THOUGHT, LET'S PASS ON THAT.
YOU SHOULD HAVE BARGAINED, JABBA...

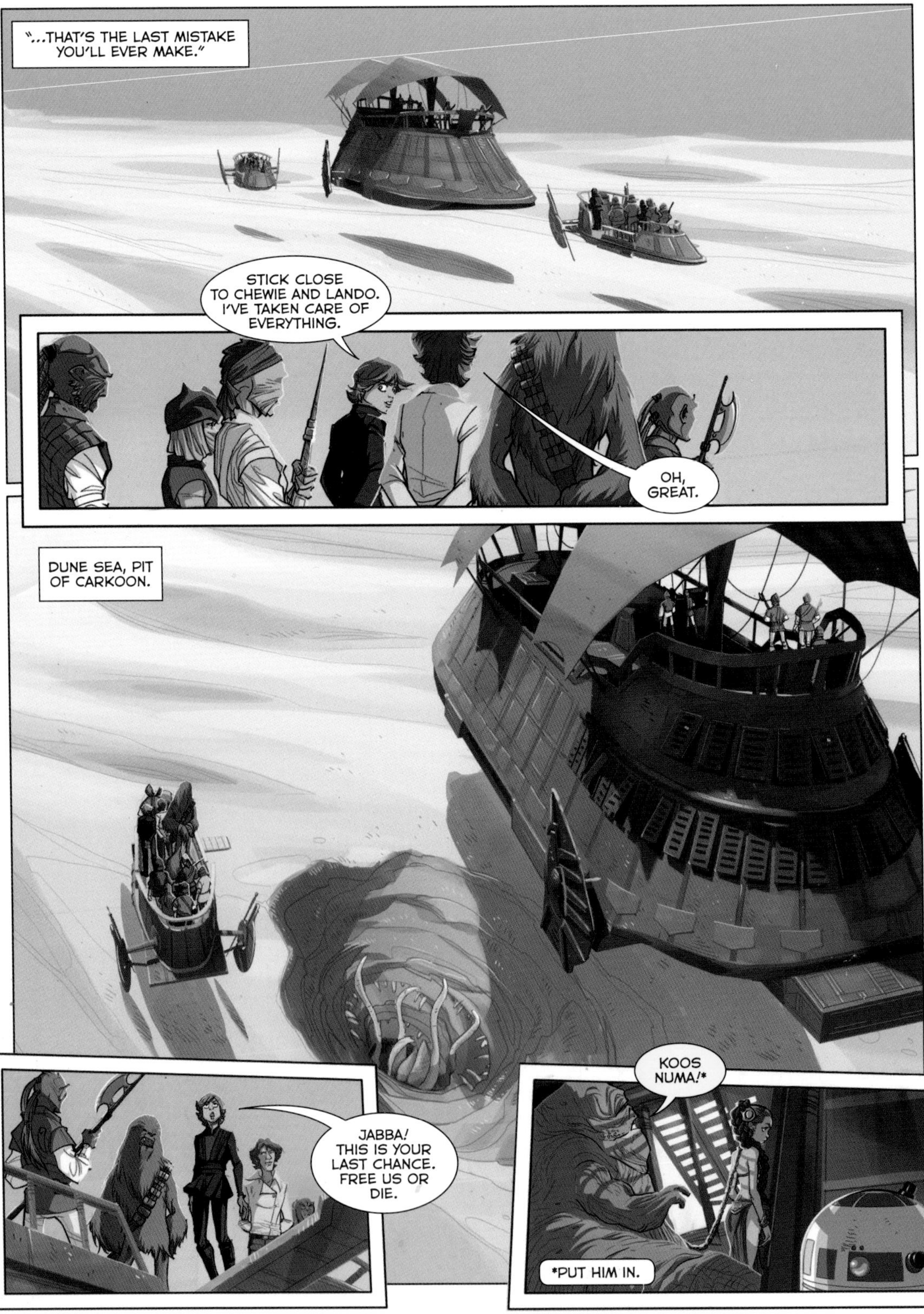
"...THAT'S THE LAST MISTAKE YOU'LL EVER MAKE."
STICK CLOSE TO CHEWIE AND LANDO. I'VE TAKEN CARE OF EVERYTHING.
OH, GREAT.
DUNE SEA, PIT OF CARKOON.
JABBA! THIS IS YOUR LAST CHANCE. FREE US OR DIE.
KOOS NUMA!*
*PUT HIM IN.

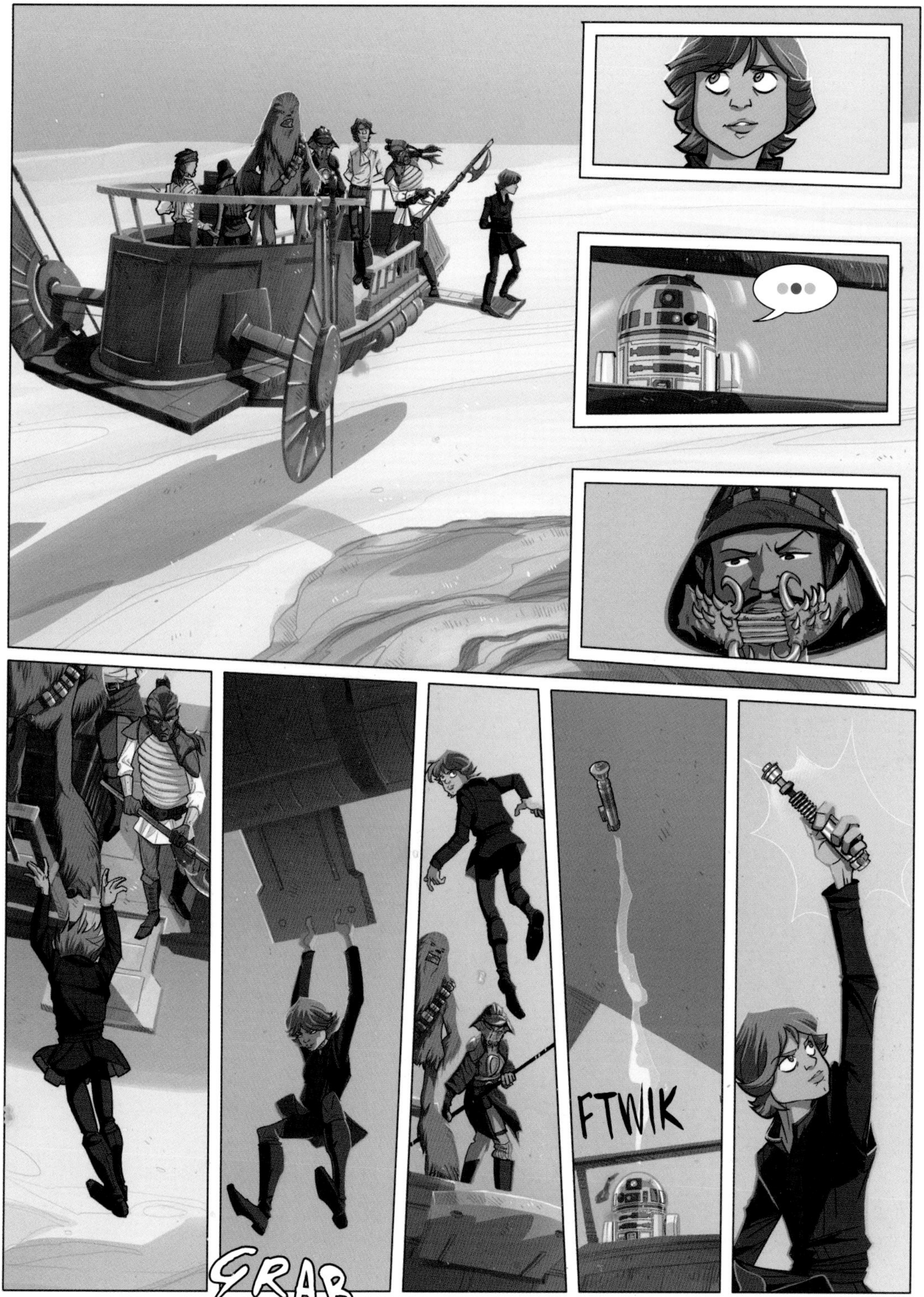
GRAB
FTWIK

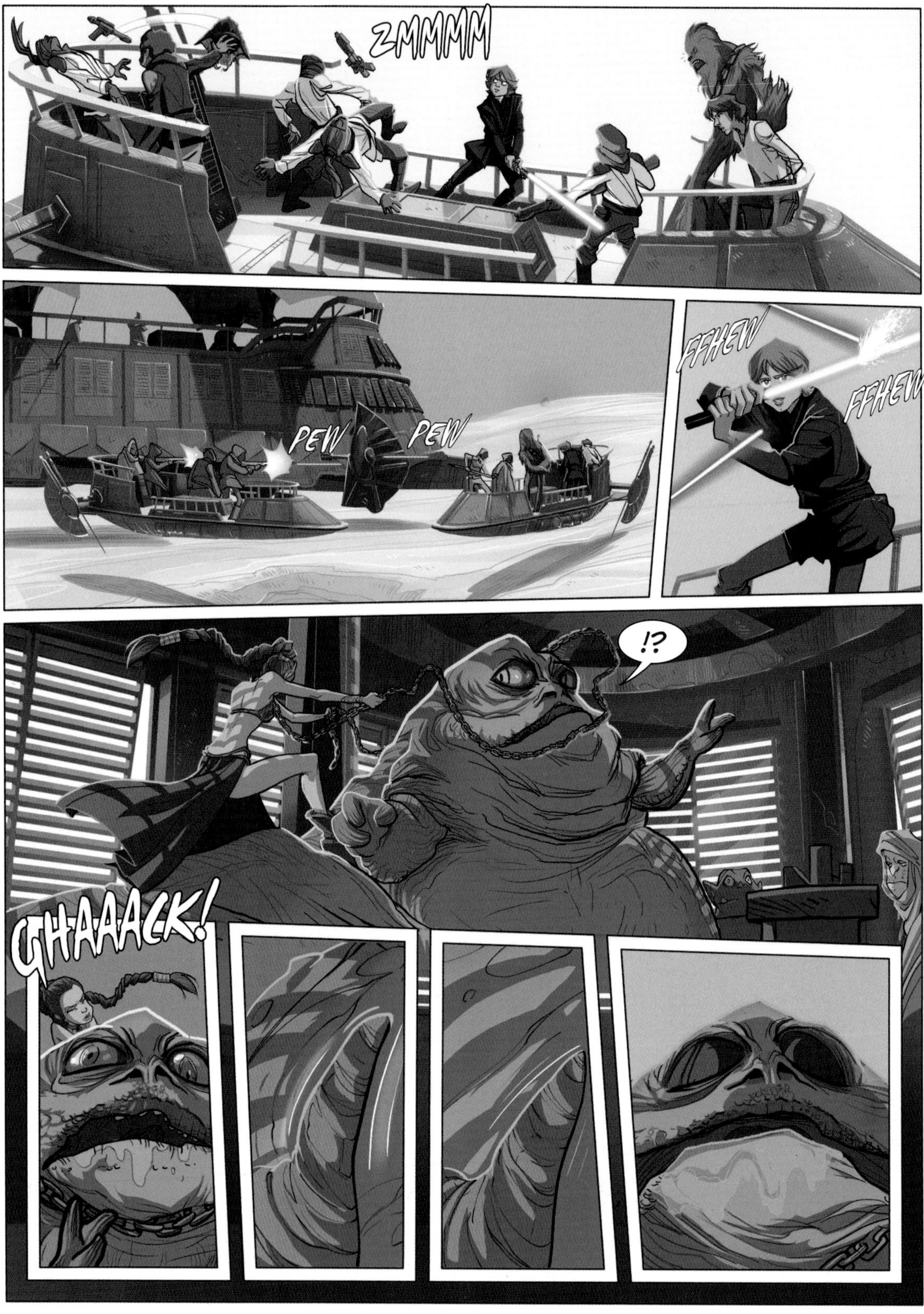
ZMMMM
PEW
PEW
FFHEW
FFHEW
!?
GHAAACK!

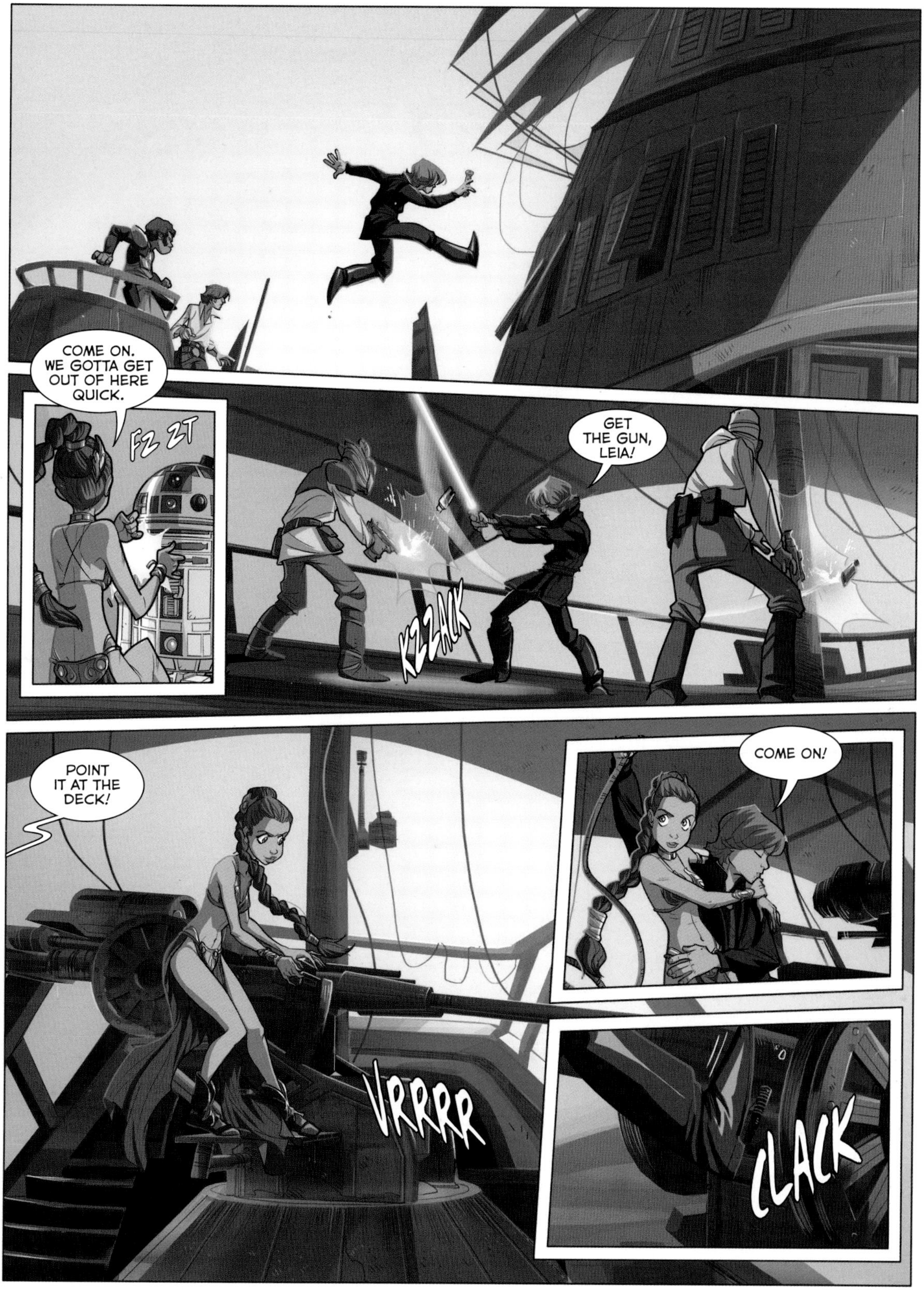
COME ON. WE GOTTA GET OUT OF HERE QUICK.
FZ ZT
GET THE GUN, LEIA!
KZZACK
POINT IT AT THE DECK!
COME ON!
VRRRR
CLACK

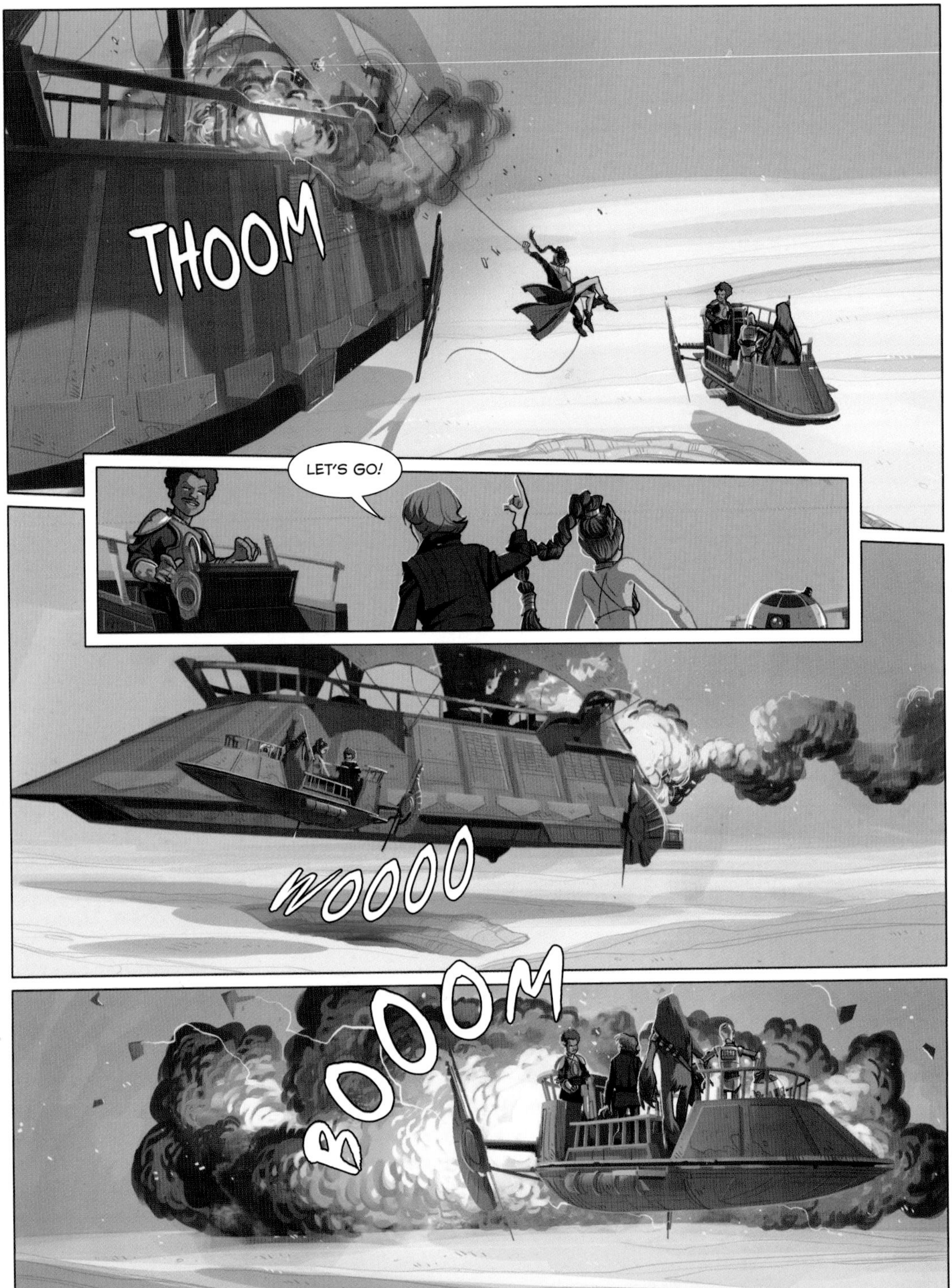
THOOM
LET'S GO!
WOOOO
BOOOOM

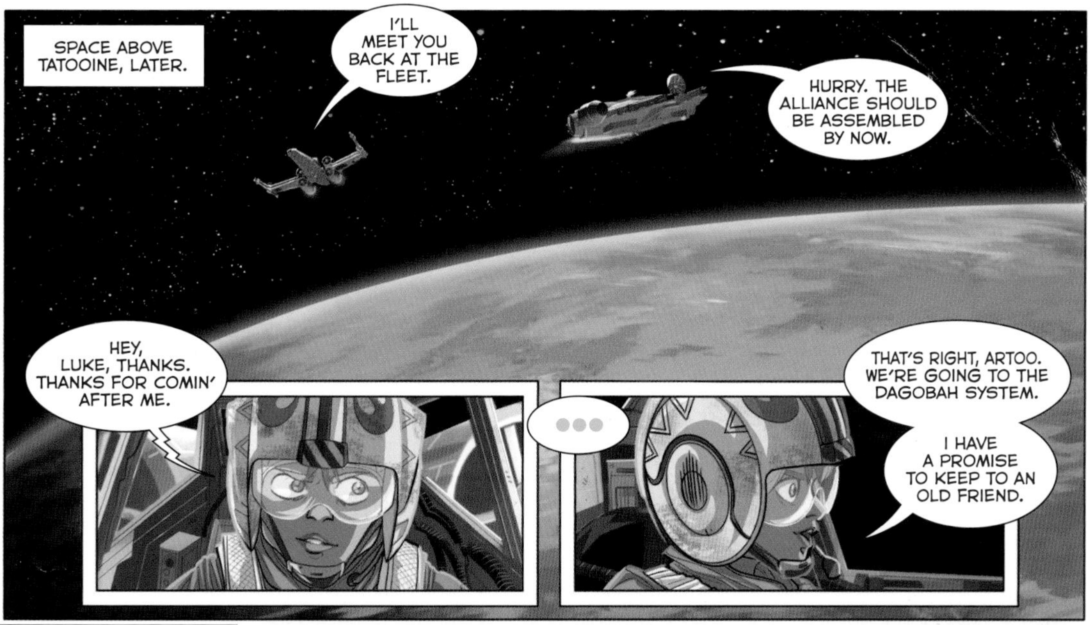
SPACE ABOVE TATOOINE, LATER.
I'LL MEET YOU BACK AT THE FLEET.
HURRY. THE ALLIANCE SHOULD BE ASSEMBLED BY NOW.
HEY, LUKE, THANKS. THANKS FOR COMIN' AFTER ME.
THAT'S RIGHT, ARTOO. WE'RE GOING TO THE DAGOBAH SYSTEM.
I HAVE A PROMISE TO KEEP TO AN OLD FRIEND.

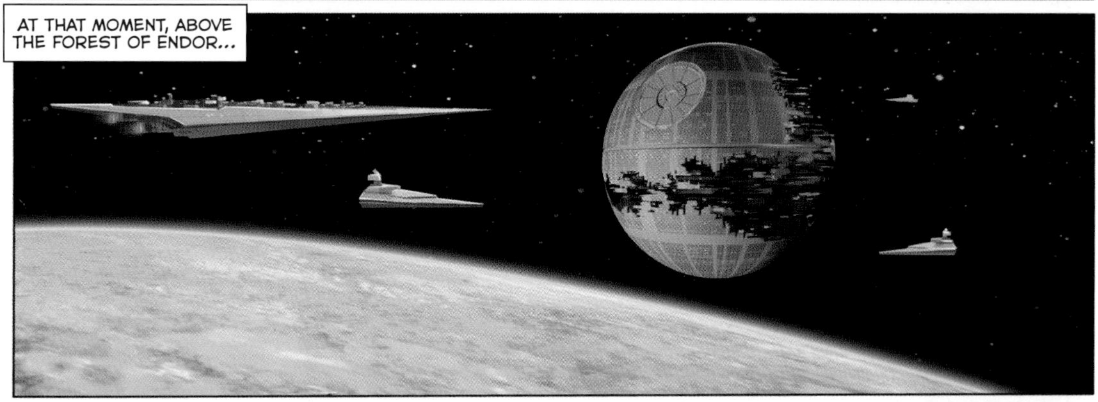
AT THAT MOMENT, ABOVE THE FOREST OF ENDOR...

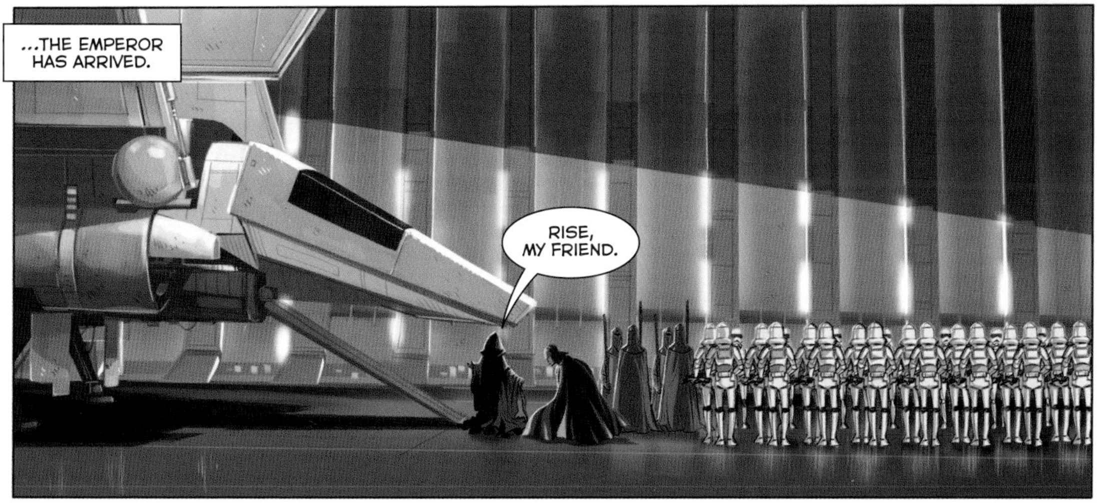
...THE EMPEROR HAS ARRIVED.
RISE, MY FRIEND.

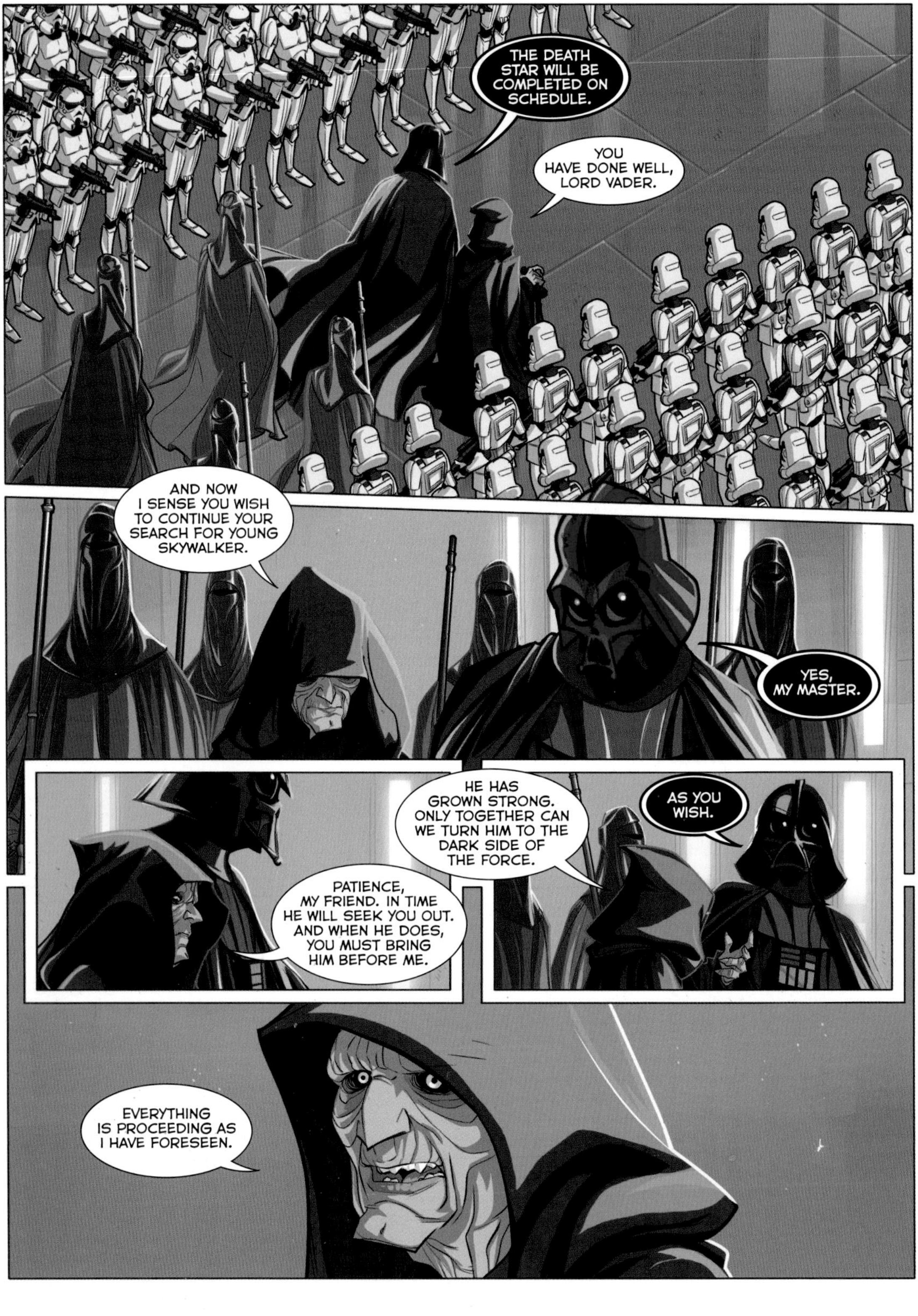
THE DEATH STAR WILL BE COMPLETED ON SCHEDULE.
YOU HAVE DONE WELL, LORD VADER.
AND NOW I SENSE YOU WISH TO CONTINUE YOUR SEARCH FOR YOUNG SKYWALKER.
YES, MY MASTER.
PATIENCE, MY FRIEND. IN TIME HE WILL SEEK YOU OUT. AND WHEN HE DOES, YOU MUST BRING HIM BEFORE ME.
AS YOU WISH.
HE HAS GROWN STRONG. ONLY TOGETHER CAN WE TURN HIM TO THE DARK SIDE OF THE FORCE.
EVERYTHING IS PROCEEDING AS I HAVE FORESEEN.

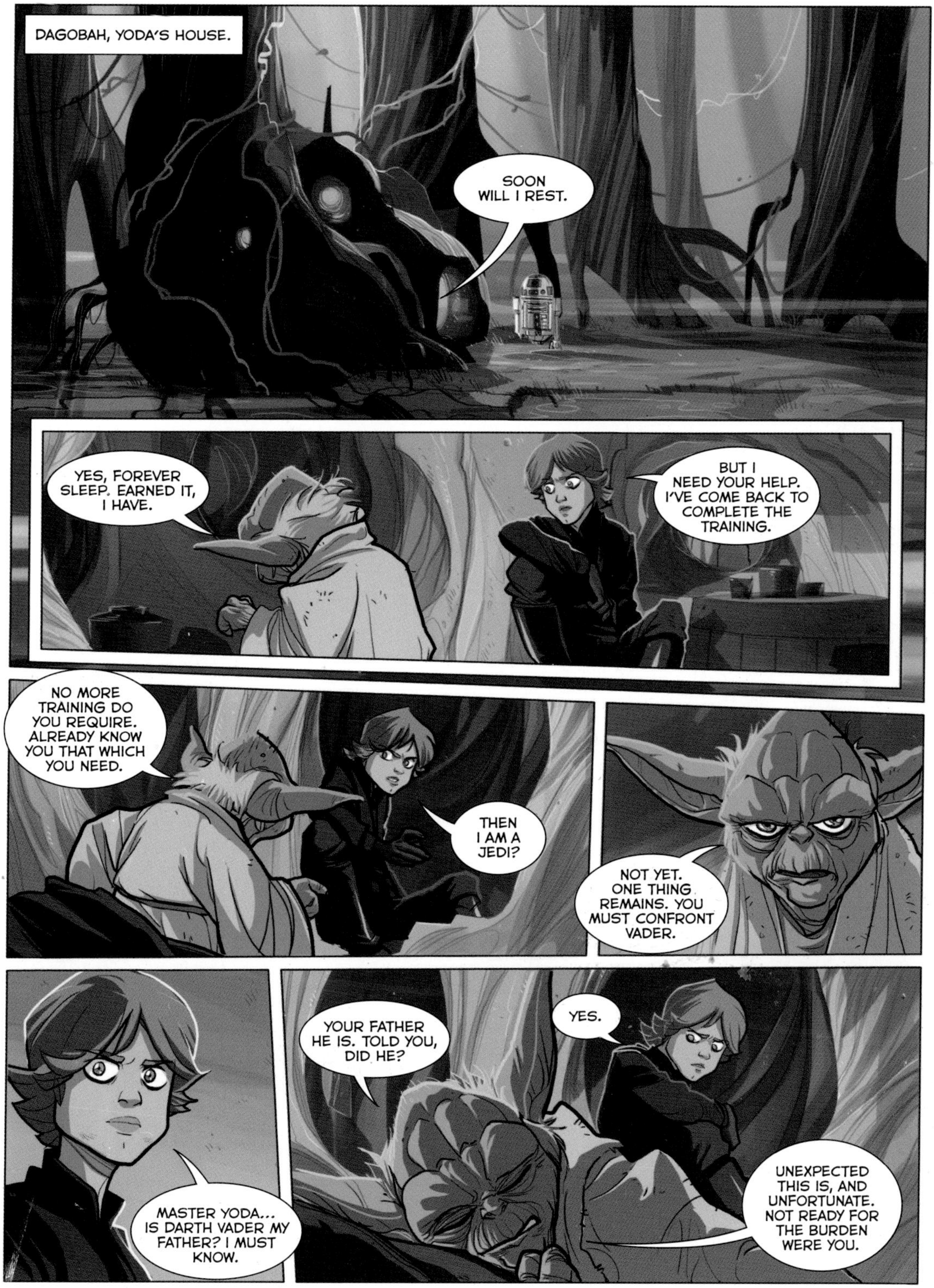
DAGOBAH, YODA'S HOUSE.
SOON WILL I REST.
YES, FOREVER SLEEP. EARNED IT, I HAVE.
BUT I NEED YOUR HELP. I'VE COME BACK TO COMPLETE THE TRAINING.
NO MORE TRAINING DO YOU REQUIRE. ALREADY KNOW YOU THAT WHICH YOU NEED.
THEN I AM A JEDI?
NOT YET. ONE THING REMAINS. YOU MUST CONFRONT VADER.
MASTER YODA... IS DARTH VADER MY FATHER? I MUST KNOW.
YOUR FATHER HE IS. TOLD YOU, DID HE?
YES.
UNEXPECTED THIS IS, AND UNFORTUNATE. NOT READY FOR THE BURDEN WERE YOU.

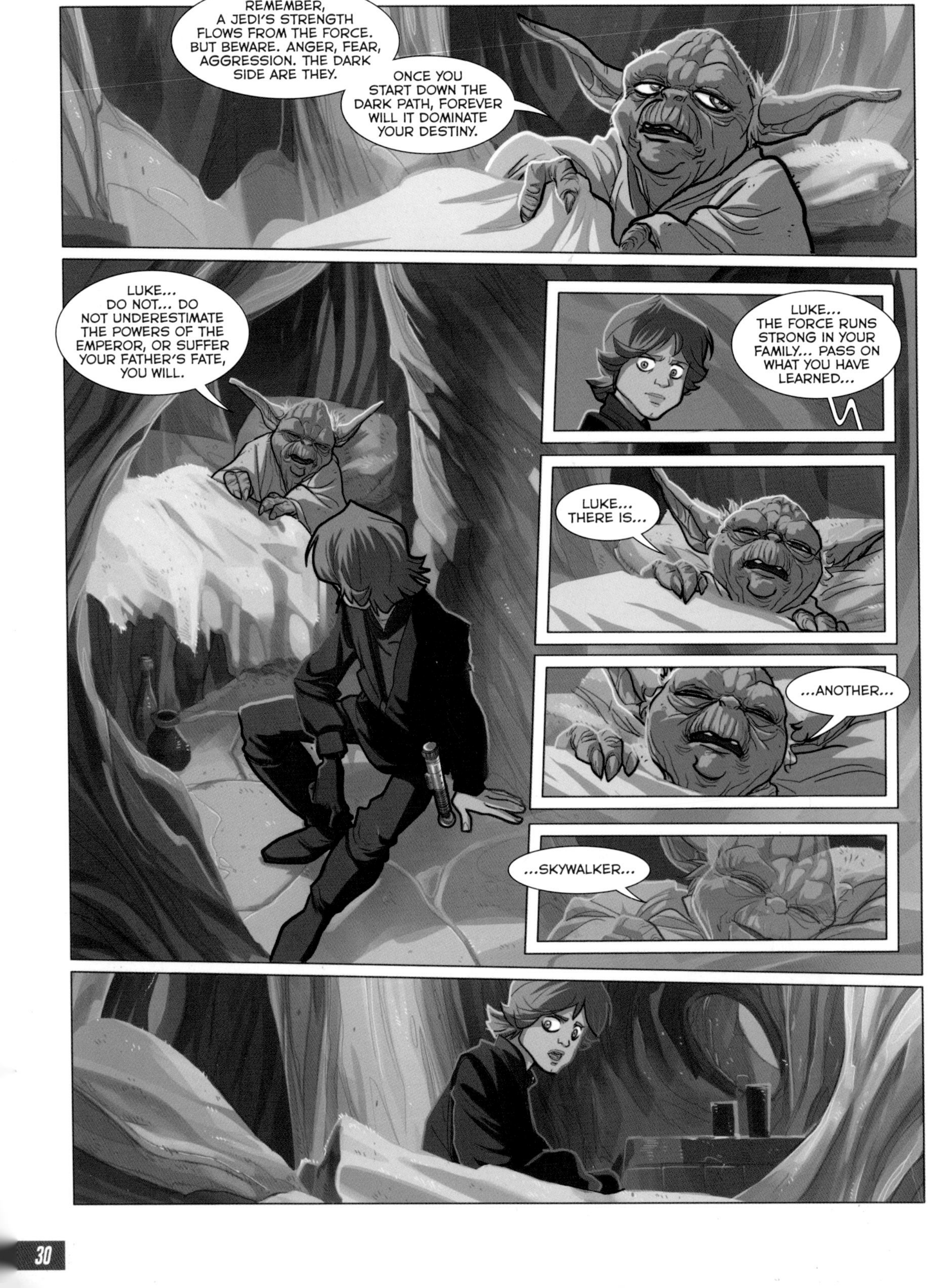
REMEMBER, A JEDI'S STRENGTH FLOWS FROM THE FORCE. BUT BEWARE. ANGER, FEAR, AGGRESSION. THE DARK SIDE ARE THEY.
ONCE YOU START DOWN THE DARK PATH, FOREVER WILL IT DOMINATE YOUR DESTINY.
LUKE... DO NOT... DO NOT UNDERESTIMATE THE POWERS OF THE EMPEROR, OR SUFFER YOUR FATHER'S FATE, YOU WILL.
LUKE... THE FORCE RUNS STRONG IN YOUR FAMILY... PASS ON WHAT YOU HAVE LEARNED...
LUKE... THERE IS...
...ANOTHER...
...SKYWALKER...

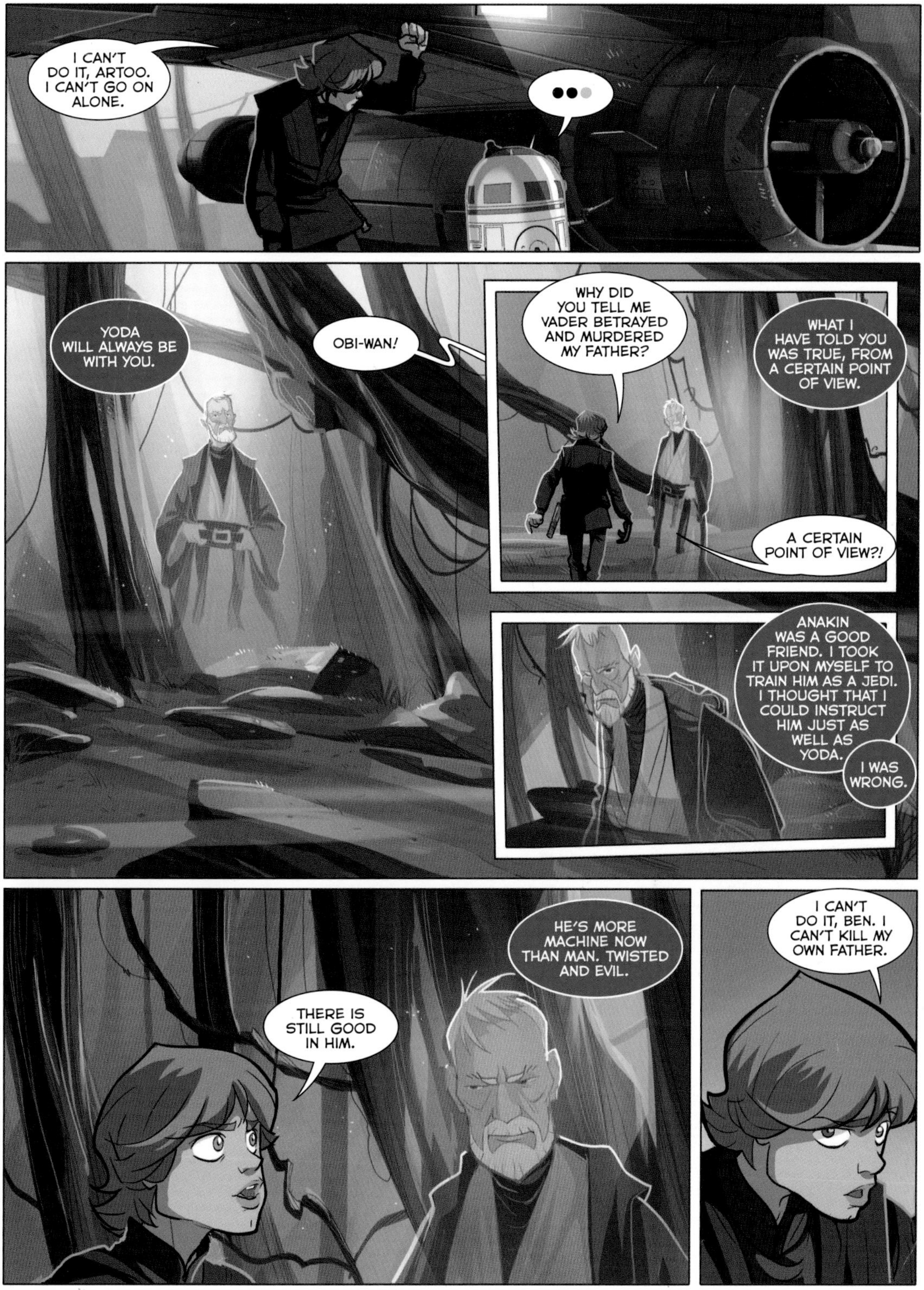

I CAN'T DO IT, ARTOO. I CAN'T GO ON ALONE.
YODA WILL ALWAYS BE WITH YOU.
OBI-WAN!
WHY DID YOU TELL ME VADER BETRAYED AND MURDERED MY FATHER?
WHAT I HAVE TOLD YOU WAS TRUE, FROM A CERTAIN POINT OF VIEW.
A CERTAIN POINT OF VIEW?!
ANAKIN WAS A GOOD FRIEND. I TOOK IT UPON MYSELF TO TRAIN HIM AS A JEDI. I THOUGHT THAT I COULD INSTRUCT HIM JUST AS WELL AS YODA.
I WAS WRONG.
HE'S MORE MACHINE NOW THAN MAN. TWISTED AND EVIL.
THERE IS STILL GOOD IN HIM.
I CAN'T DO IT, BEN. I CAN'T KILL MY OWN FATHER.

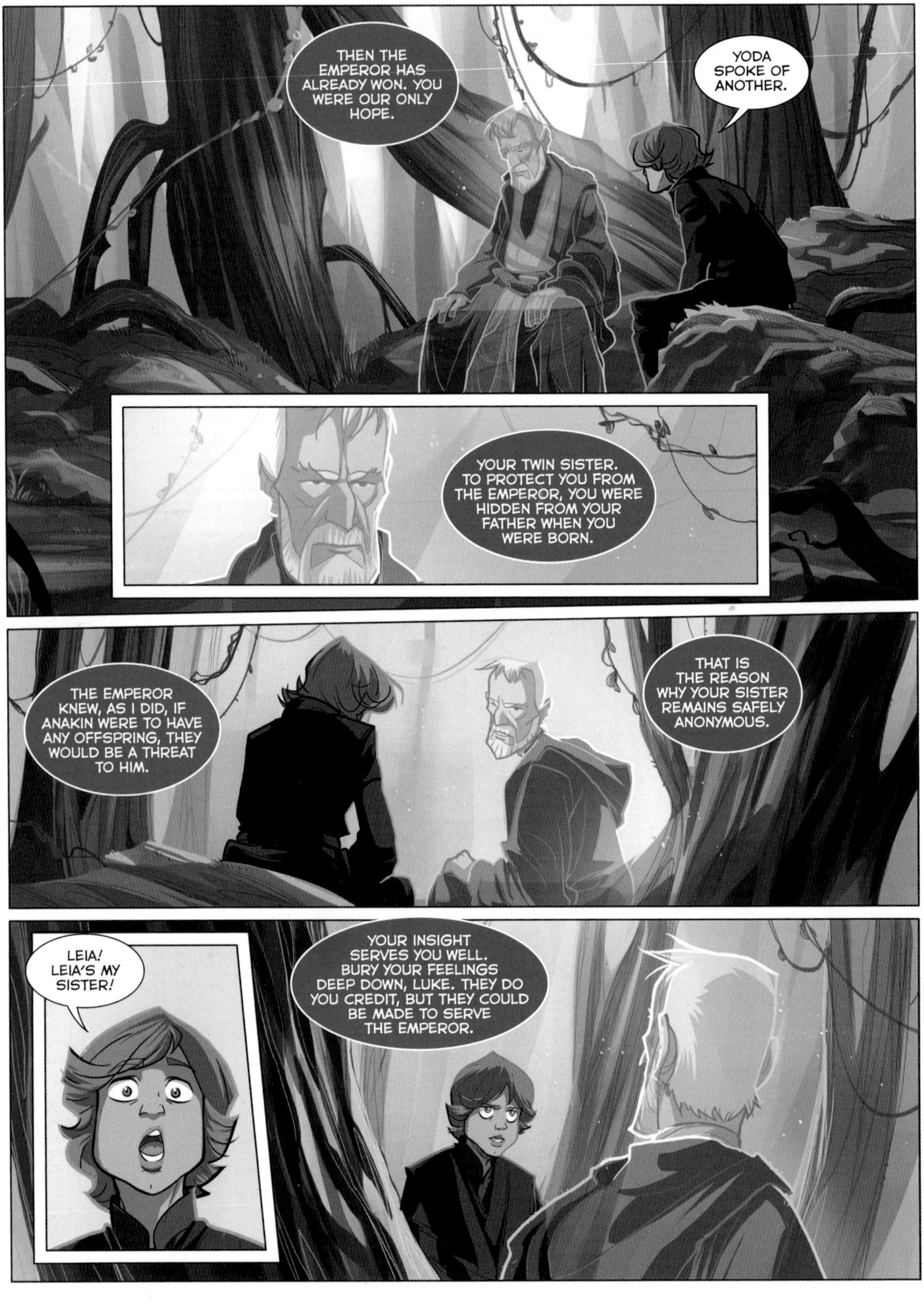
THEN THE EMPEROR HAS ALREADY WON. YOU WERE OUR ONLY HOPE.
YODA SPOKE OF ANOTHER.
YOUR TWIN SISTER. TO PROTECT YOU FROM THE EMPEROR, YOU WERE HIDDEN FROM YOUR FATHER WHEN YOU WERE BORN.
THE EMPEROR KNEW, AS I DID, IF ANAKIN WERE TO HAVE ANY OFFSPRING, THEY WOULD BE A THREAT TO HIM.
THAT IS THE REASON WHY YOUR SISTER REMAINS SAFELY ANONYMOUS.
LEIA! LEIA'S MY SISTER!
YOUR INSIGHT SERVES YOU WELL. BURY YOUR FEELINGS DEEP DOWN, LUKE. THEY DO YOU CREDIT, BUT THEY COULD BE MADE TO SERVE THE EMPEROR.

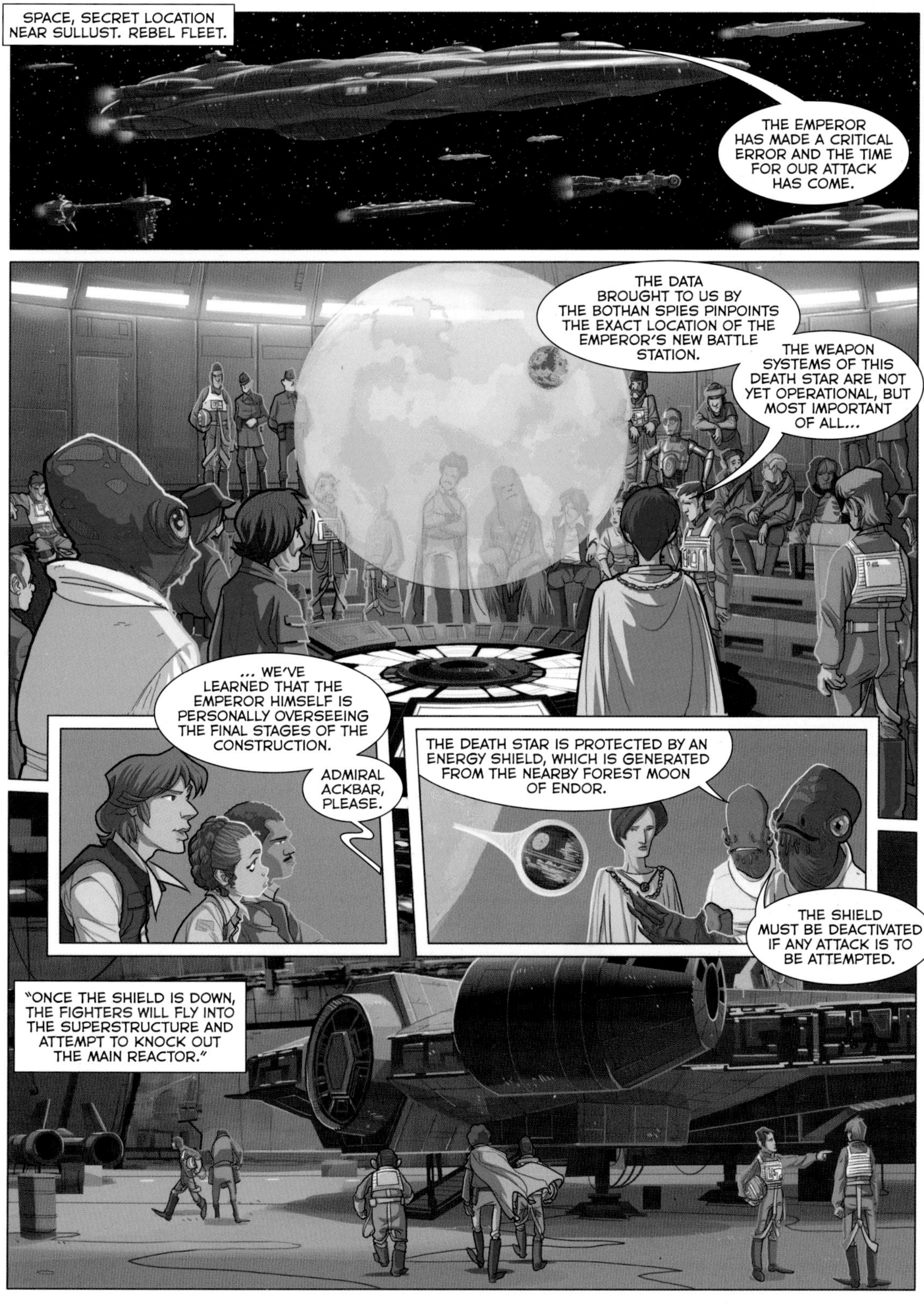

SPACE, SECRET LOCATION NEAR SULLUST. REBEL FLEET.
THE EMPEROR HAS MADE A CRITICAL ERROR AND THE TIME FOR OUR ATTACK HAS COME.
THE DATA BROUGHT TO US BY THE BOTHAN SPIES PINPOINTS THE EXACT LOCATION OF THE EMPEROR'S NEW BATTLE STATION.
THE WEAPON SYSTEMS OF THIS DEATH STAR ARE NOT YET OPERATIONAL, BUT MOST IMPORTANT OF ALL...
... WE'VE LEARNED THAT THE EMPEROR HIMSELF IS PERSONALLY OVERSEEING THE FINAL STAGES OF THE CONSTRUCTION.
ADMIRAL ACKBAR, PLEASE.
THE DEATH STAR IS PROTECTED BY AN ENERGY SHIELD, WHICH IS GENERATED FROM THE NEARBY FOREST MOON OF ENDOR.
THE SHIELD MUST BE DEACTIVATED IF ANY ATTACK IS TO BE ATTEMPTED.
"ONCE THE SHIELD IS DOWN, THE FIGHTERS WILL FLY INTO THE SUPERSTRUCTURE AND ATTEMPT TO KNOCK OUT THE MAIN REACTOR."

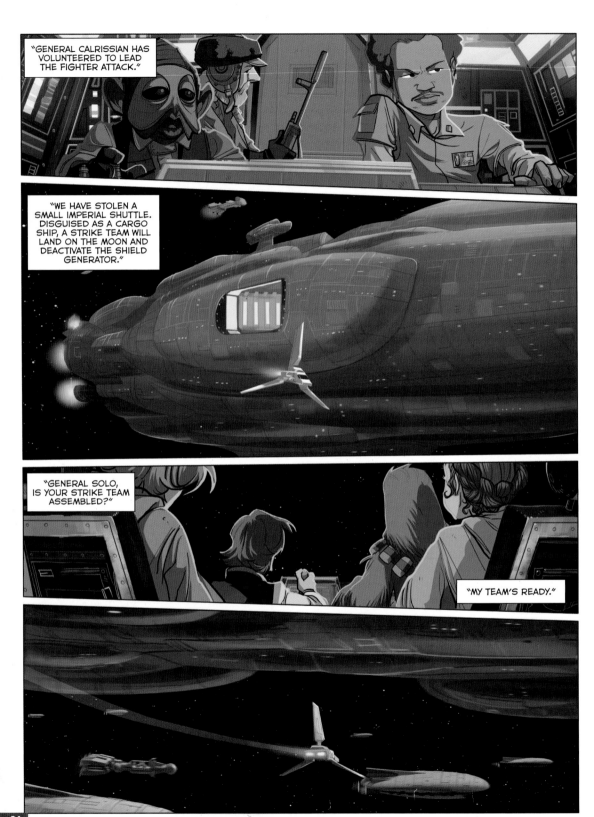

"GENERAL CALRISSIAN HAS VOLUNTEERED TO LEAD THE FIGHTER ATTACK."

"WE HAVE STOLEN A SMALL IMPERIAL SHUTTLE. DISGUISED AS A CARGO SHIP, A STRIKE TEAM WILL LAND ON THE MOON AND DEACTIVATE THE SHIELD GENERATOR."

"GENERAL SOLO, IS YOUR STRIKE TEAM ASSEMBLED?"

"MY TEAM'S READY."

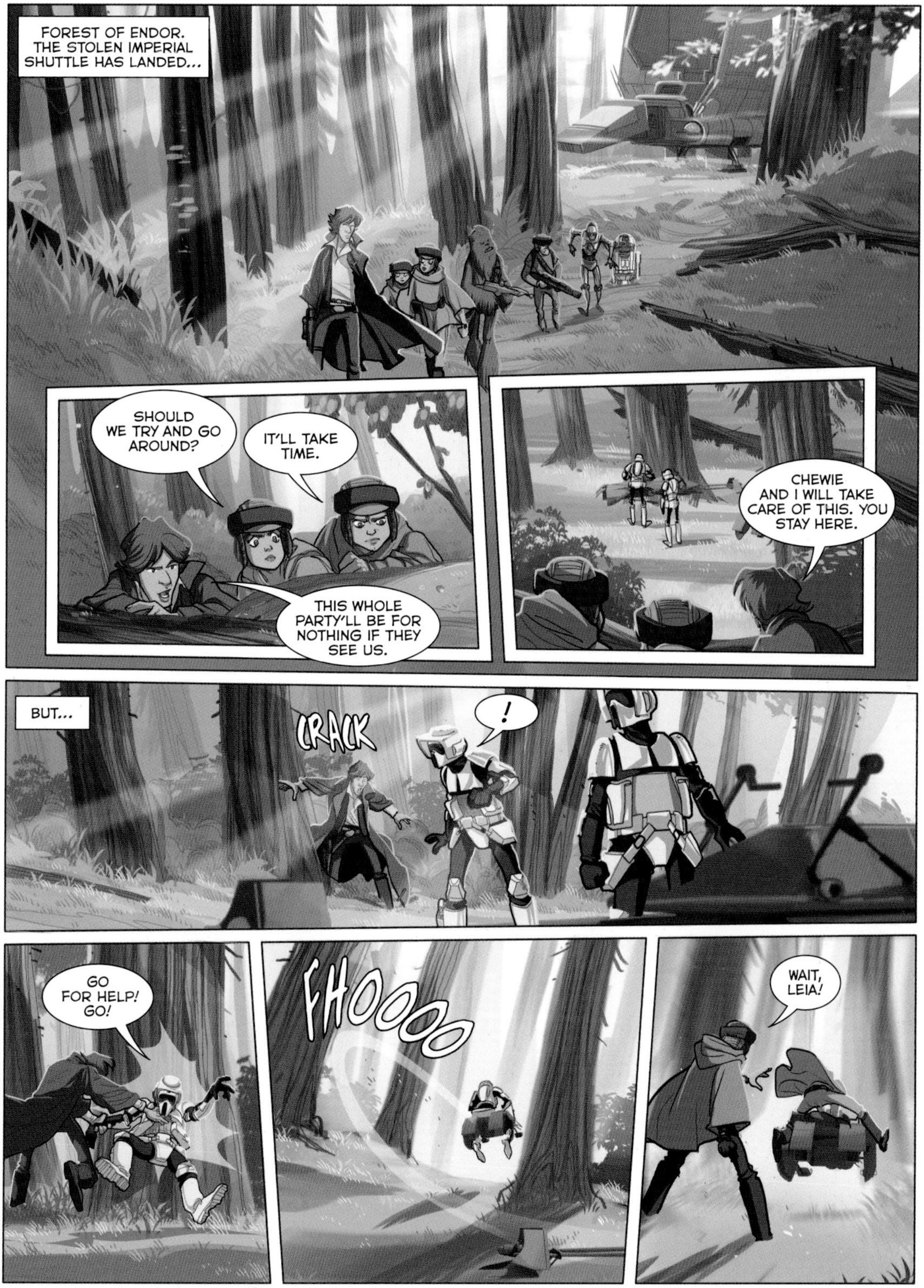
FOREST OF ENDOR. THE STOLEN IMPERIAL SHUTTLE HAS LANDED...
SHOULD WE TRY AND GO AROUND?
IT'LL TAKE TIME.
THIS WHOLE PARTY'LL BE FOR NOTHING IF THEY SEE US.
CHEWIE AND I WILL TAKE CARE OF THIS. YOU STAY HERE.
BUT...
CRACK
!
GO FOR HELP! GO!
FHOOOO
WAIT, LEIA!

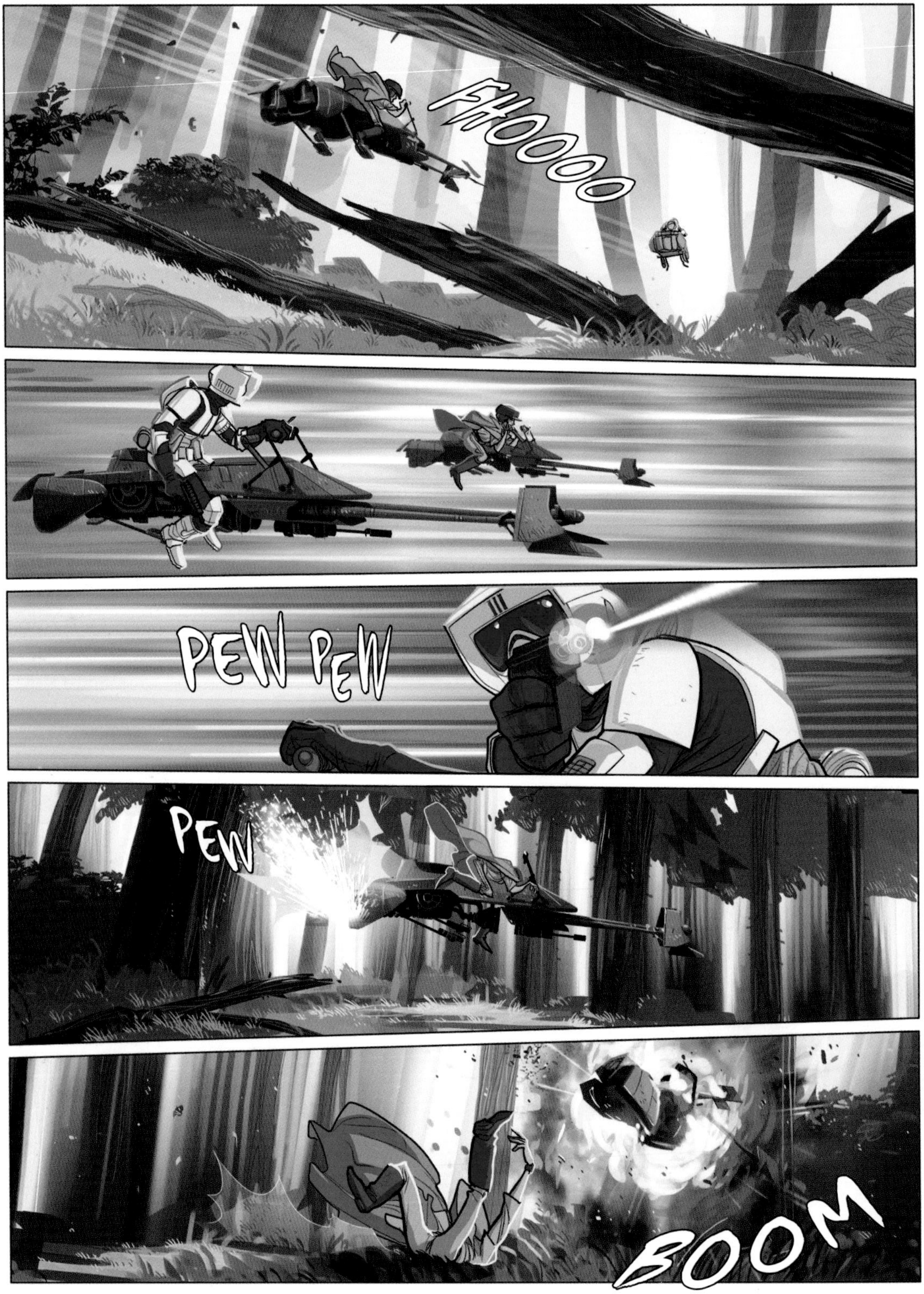
FHOOOO
PEW PEW
PEW
BOOM

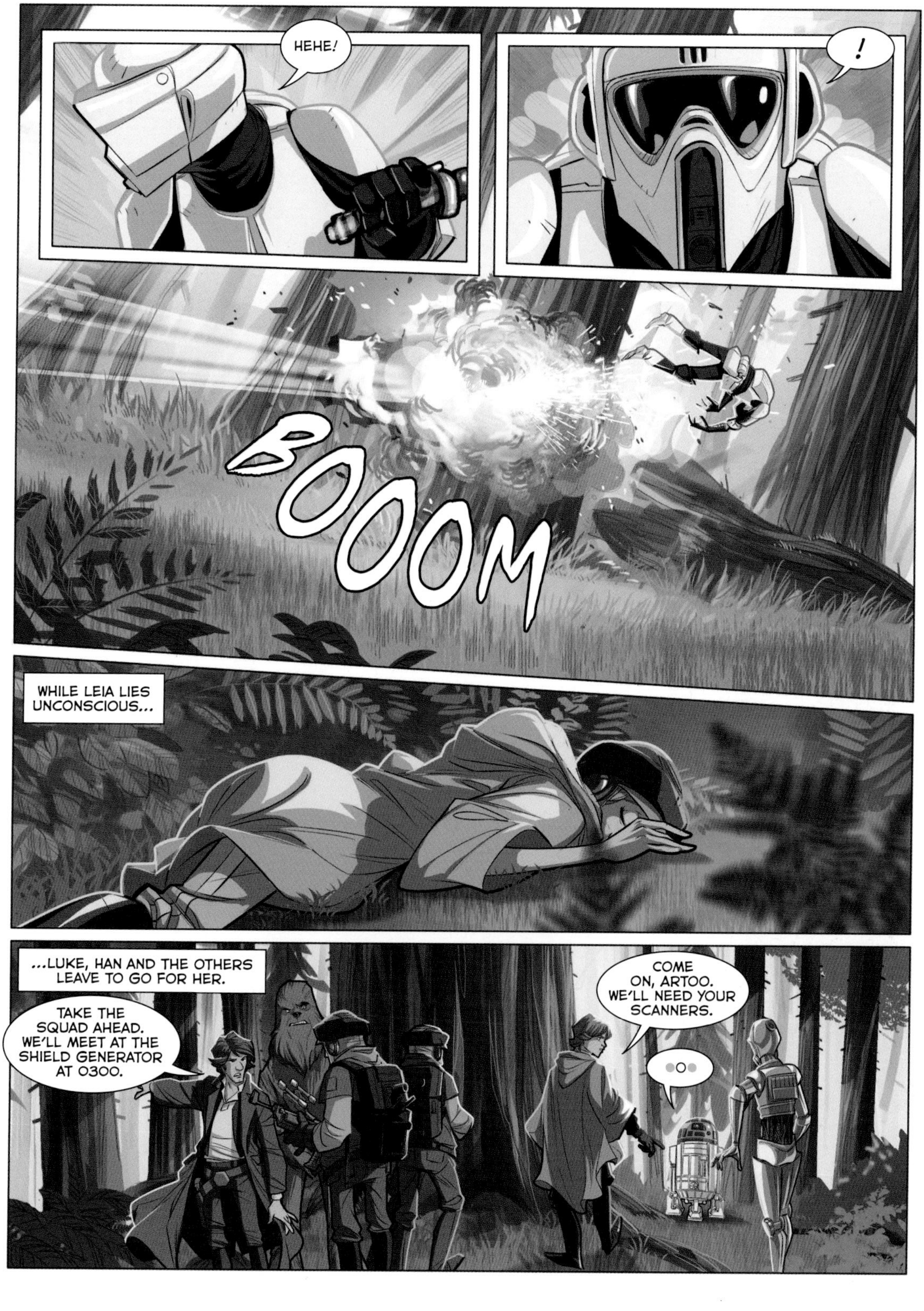

HEHE!
!
BOOOM
WHILE LEIA LIES UNCONSCIOUS...
...LUKE, HAN AND THE OTHERS LEAVE TO GO FOR HER.
TAKE THE SQUAD AHEAD. WE'LL MEET AT THE SHIELD GENERATOR AT 0300.
COME ON, ARTOO. WE'LL NEED YOUR SCANNERS.

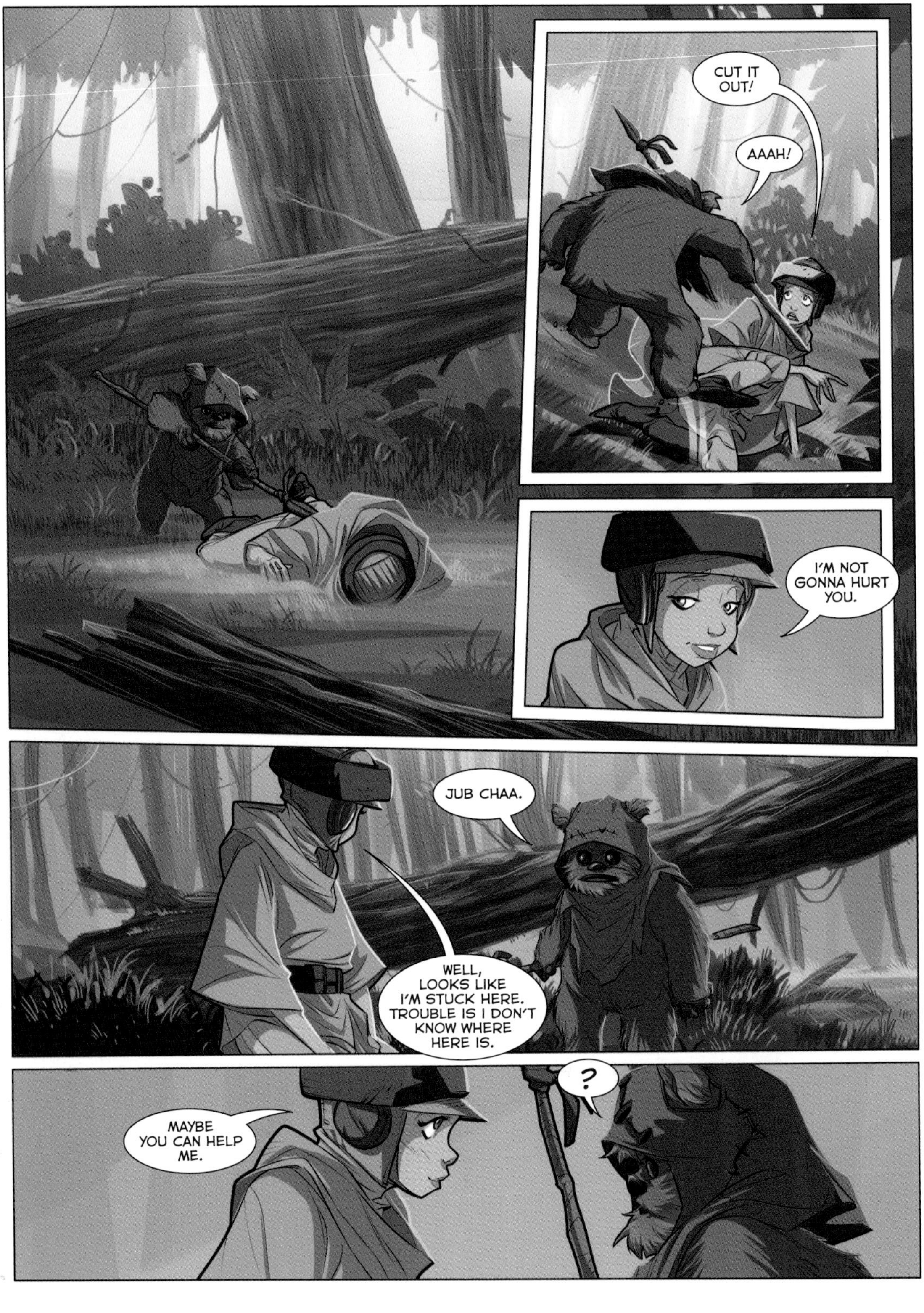
CUT IT OUT!
AAAH!
I'M NOT GONNA HURT YOU.
JUB CHAA.
WELL, LOOKS LIKE I'M STUCK HERE. TROUBLE IS I DON'T KNOW WHERE HERE IS.
MAYBE YOU CAN HELP ME.
?

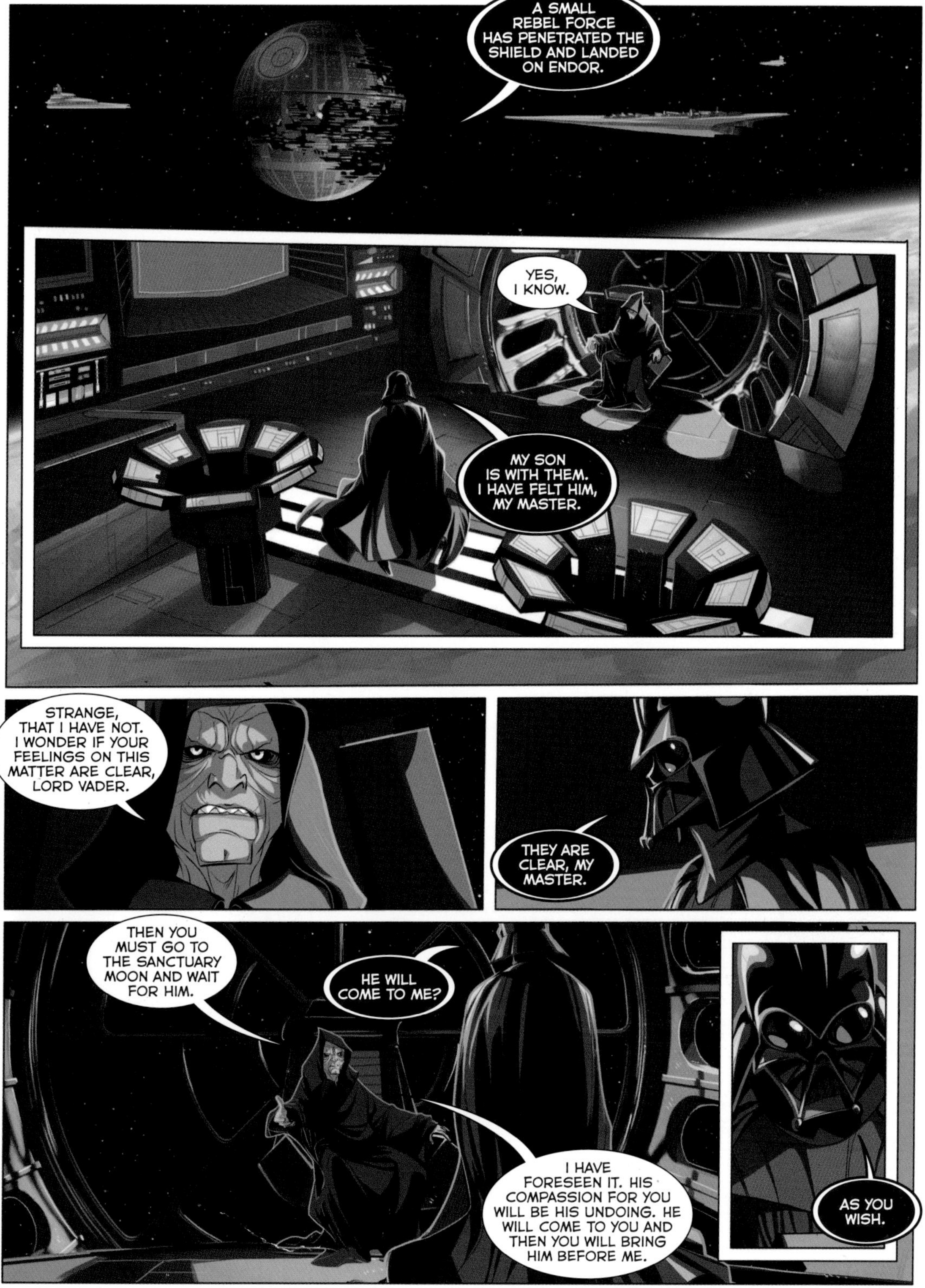
A SMALL REBEL FORCE HAS PENETRATED THE SHIELD AND LANDED ON ENDOR.
YES, I KNOW.
MY SON IS WITH THEM. I HAVE FELT HIM, MY MASTER.
STRANGE, THAT I HAVE NOT. I WONDER IF YOUR FEELINGS ON THIS MATTER ARE CLEAR, LORD VADER.
THEY ARE CLEAR, MY MASTER.
THEN YOU MUST GO TO THE SANCTUARY MOON AND WAIT FOR HIM.
HE WILL COME TO ME?
I HAVE FORESEEN IT. HIS COMPASSION FOR YOU WILL BE HIS UNDOING. HE WILL COME TO YOU AND THEN YOU WILL BRING HIM BEFORE ME.
AS YOU WISH.

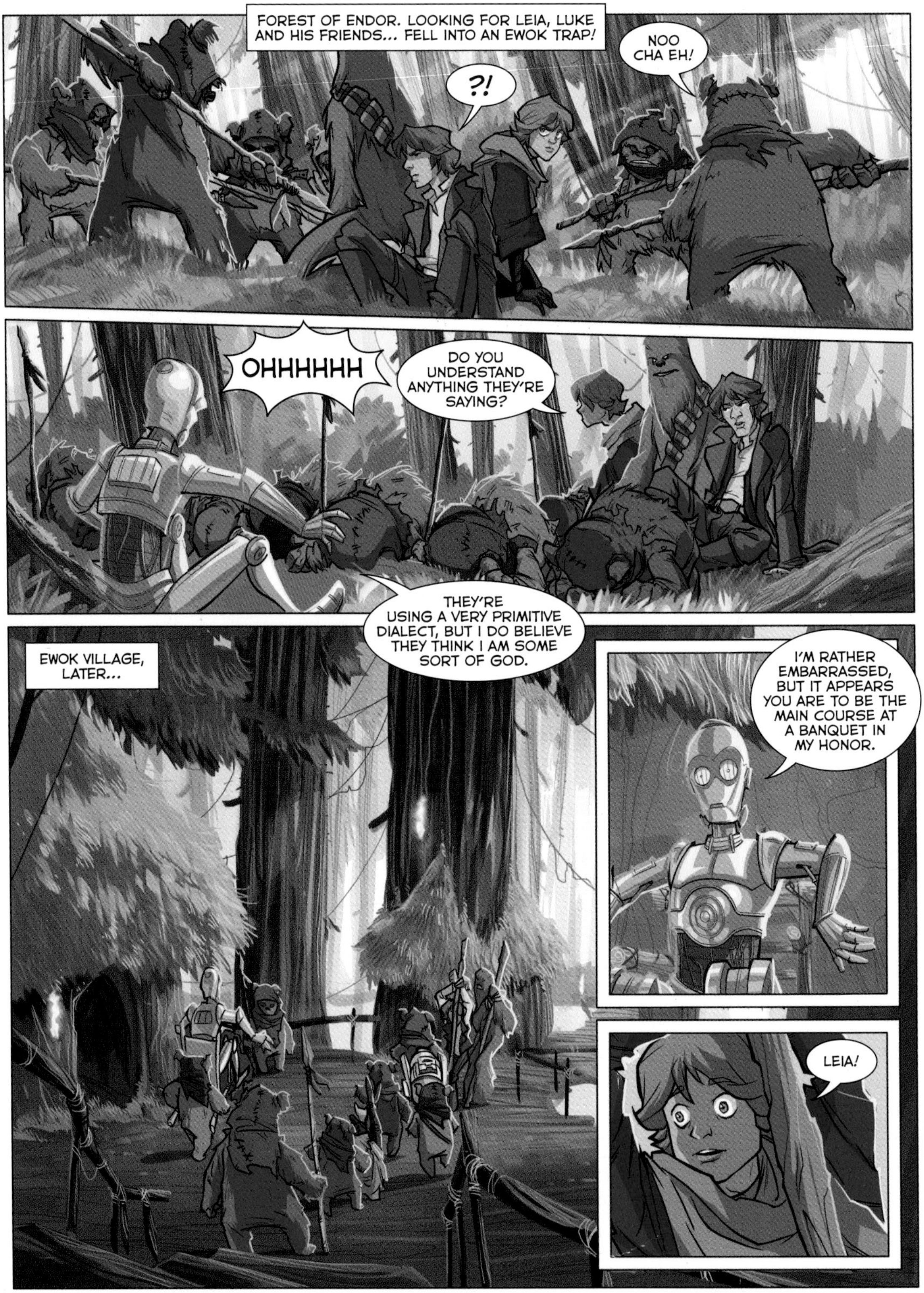
FOREST OF ENDOR. LOOKING FOR LEIA, LUKE AND HIS FRIENDS... FELL INTO AN EWOK TRAP!
?!
NOO CHA EH!
OHHHHHH
DO YOU UNDERSTAND ANYTHING THEY'RE SAYING?
THEY'RE USING A VERY PRIMITIVE DIALECT, BUT I DO BELIEVE THEY THINK I AM SOME SORT OF GOD.
EWOK VILLAGE, LATER...
I'M RATHER EMBARRASSED, BUT IT APPEARS YOU ARE TO BE THE MAIN COURSE AT A BANQUET IN MY HONOR.
LEIA!

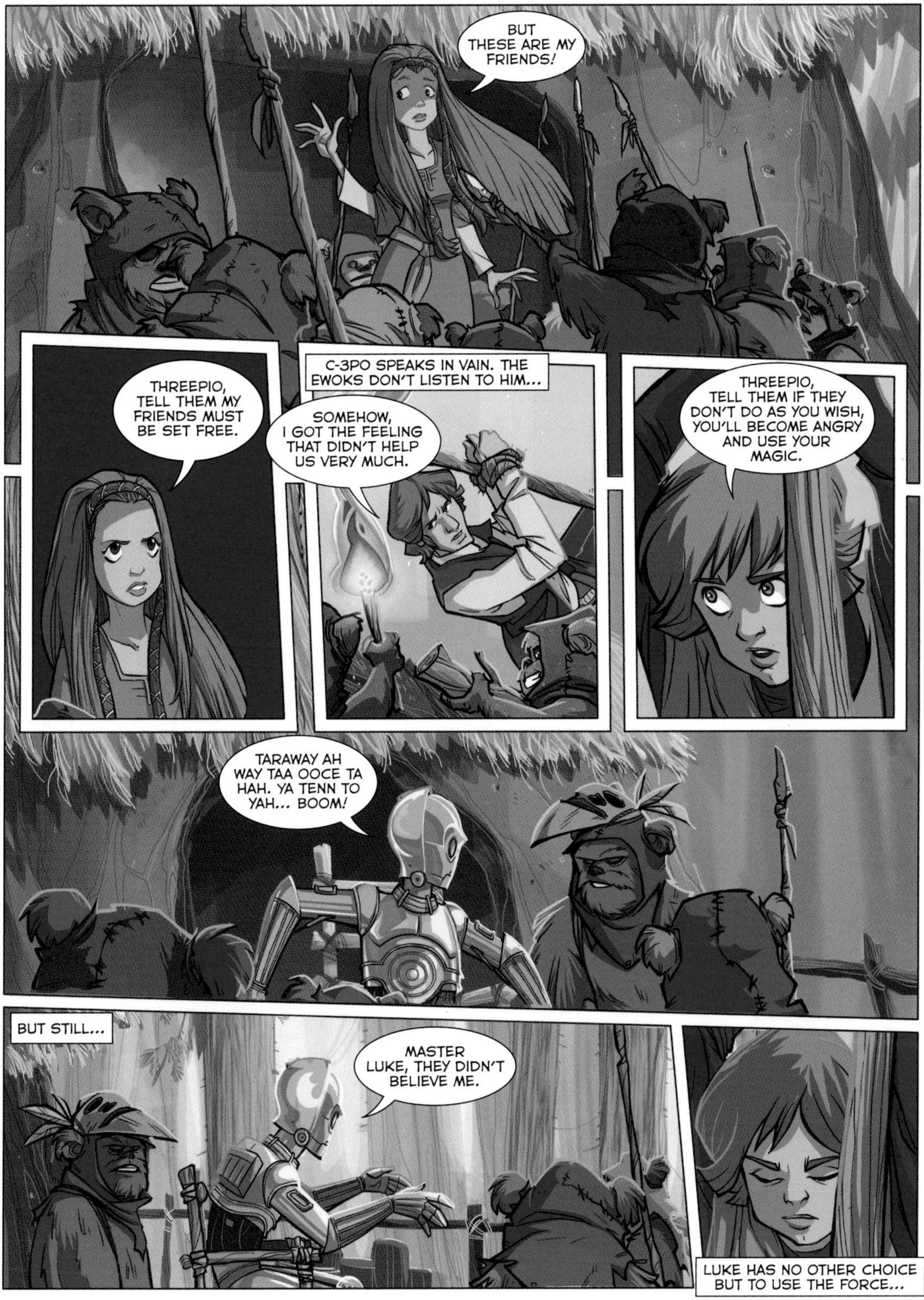
BUT THESE ARE MY FRIENDS!
THREEPIO, TELL THEM MY FRIENDS MUST BE SET FREE.
C-3PO SPEAKS IN VAIN. THE EWOKS DON'T LISTEN TO HIM...
SOMEHOW, I GOT THE FEELING THAT DIDN'T HELP US VERY MUCH.
THREEPIO, TELL THEM IF THEY DON'T DO AS YOU WISH, YOU'LL BECOME ANGRY AND USE YOUR MAGIC.
TARAWAY AH WAY TAA OOCE TA HAH. YA TENN TO YAH... BOOM!
BUT STILL...
MASTER LUKE, THEY DIDN'T BELIEVE ME.
LUKE HAS NO OTHER CHOICE BUT TO USE THE FORCE...

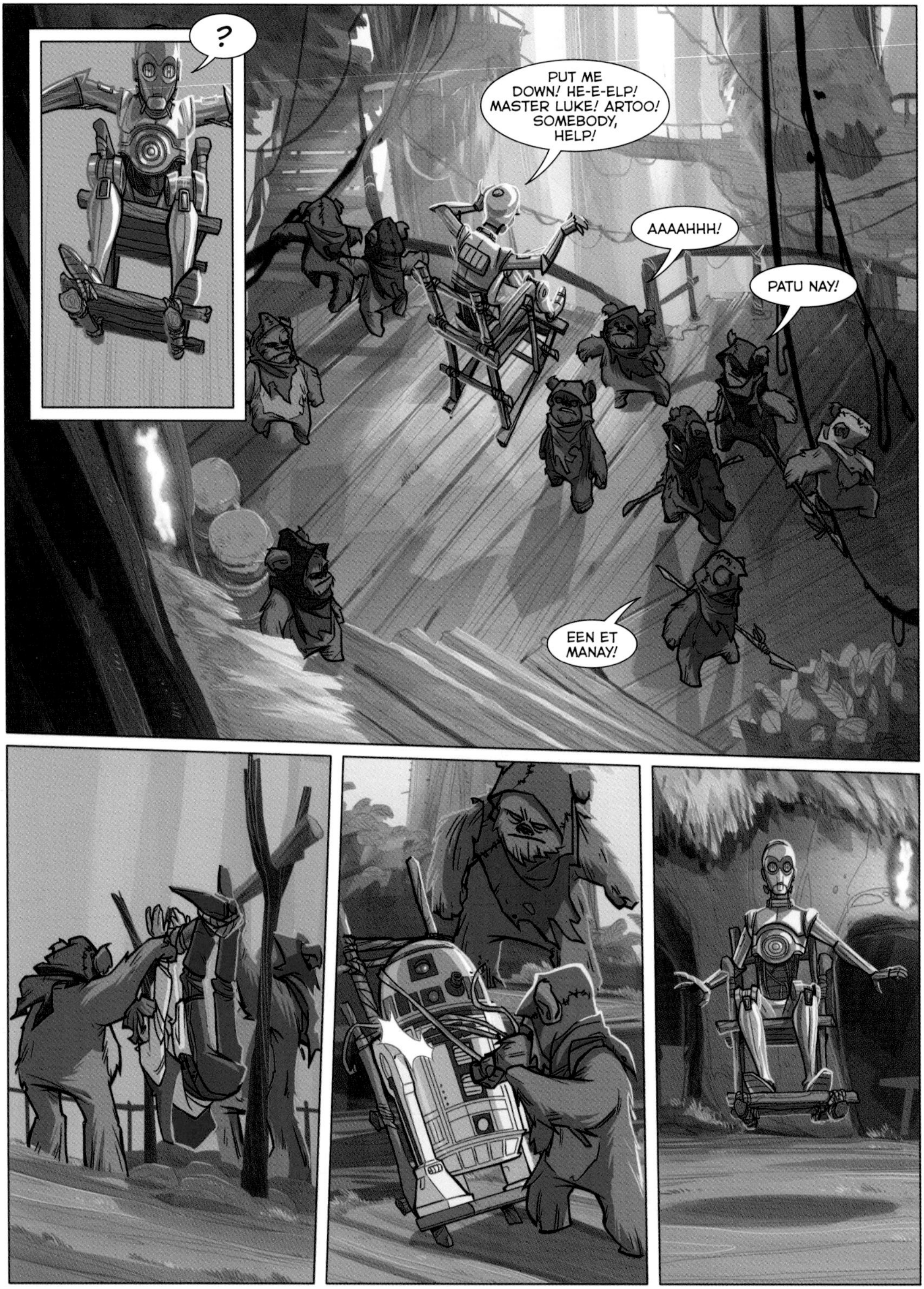
?
PUT ME DOWN! HE-E-ELP! MASTER LUKE! ARTOO! SOMEBODY, HELP!
AAAAHHH!
PATU NAY!
EEN ET MANAY!

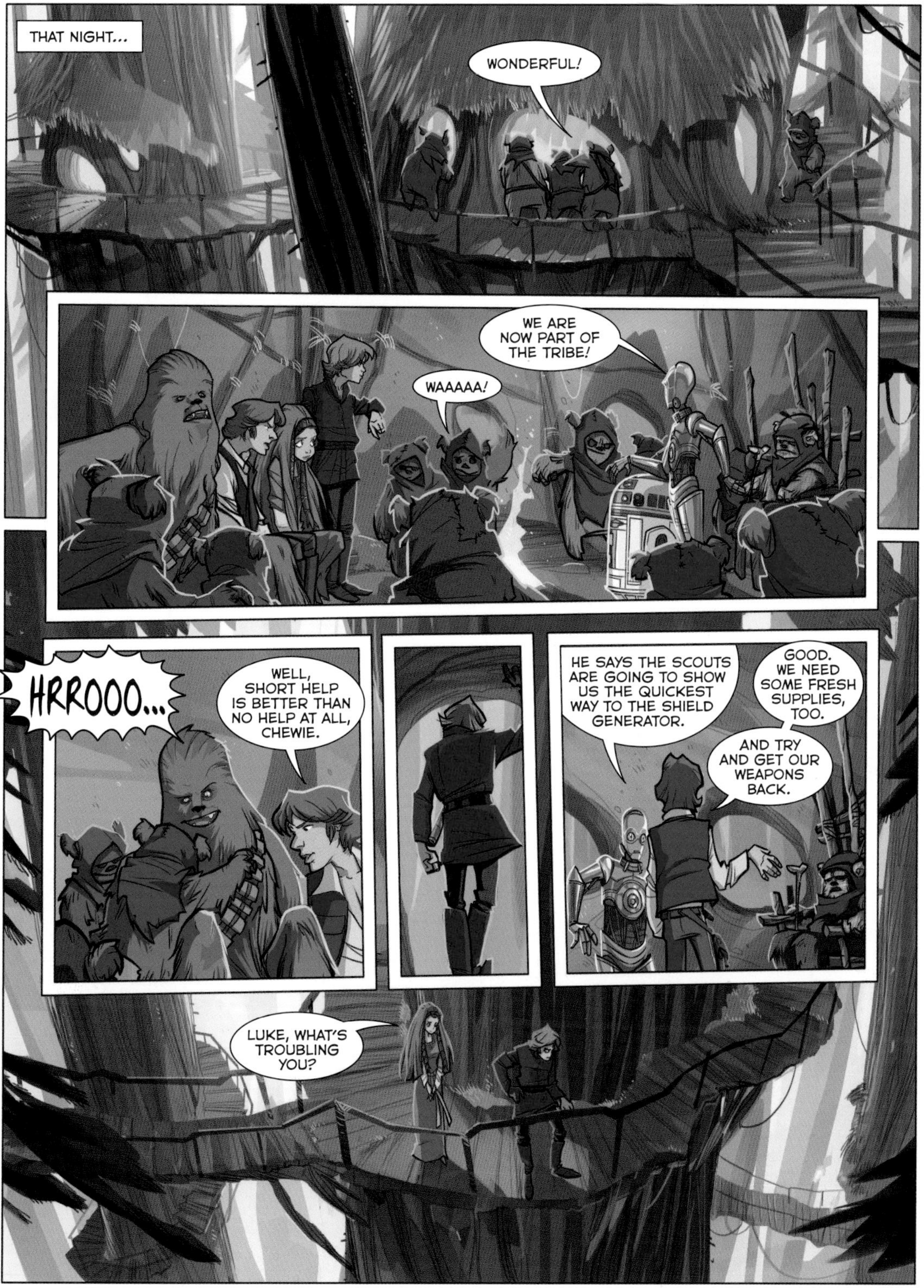
THAT NIGHT...
WONDERFUL!
WE ARE NOW PART OF THE TRIBE!
WAAAAA!
HRROOO...
WELL, SHORT HELP IS BETTER THAN NO HELP AT ALL, CHEWIE.
HE SAYS THE SCOUTS ARE GOING TO SHOW US THE QUICKEST WAY TO THE SHIELD GENERATOR.
GOOD. WE NEED SOME FRESH SUPPLIES, TOO.
AND TRY AND GET OUR WEAPONS BACK.
LUKE, WHAT'S TROUBLING YOU?

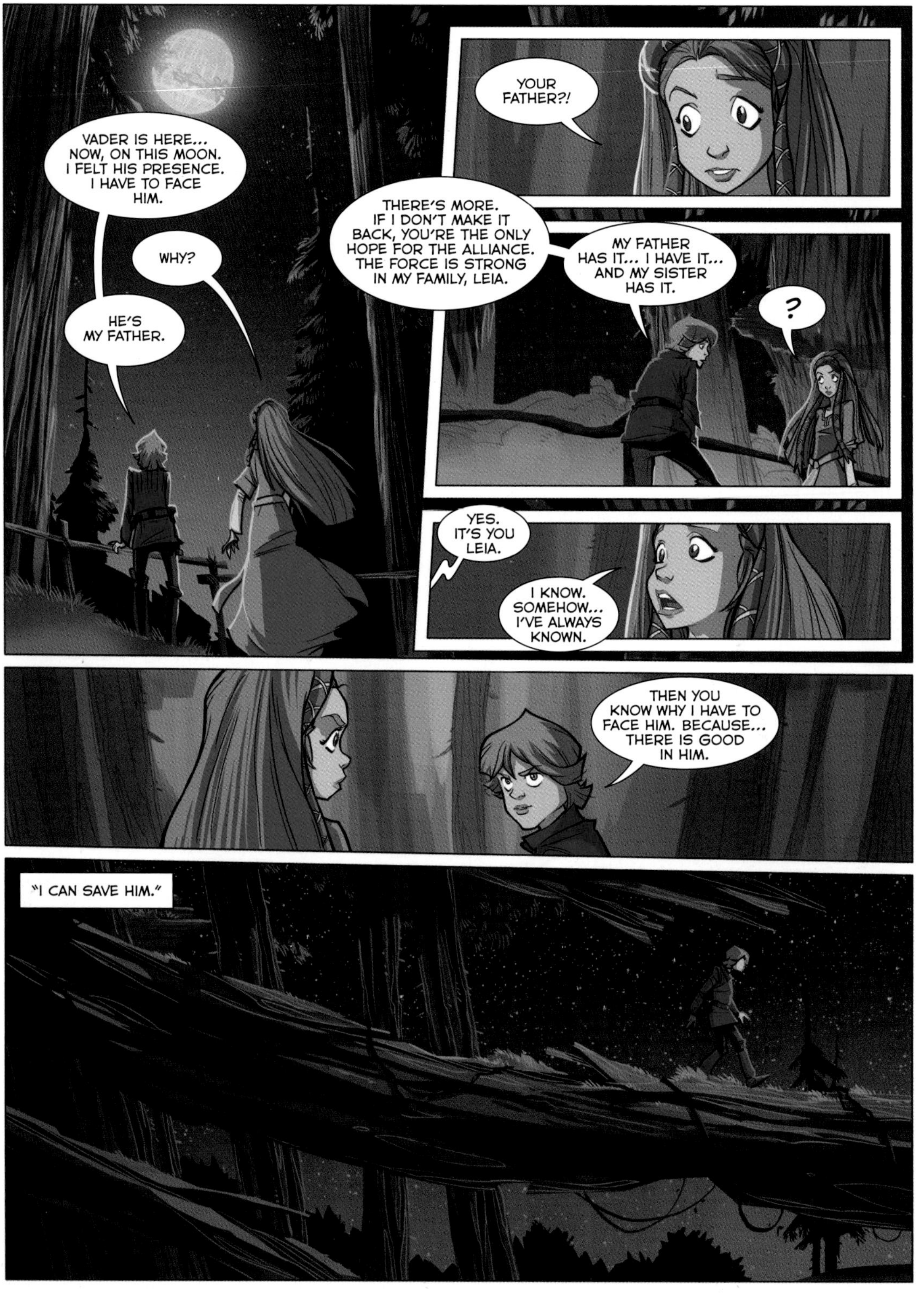
VADER IS HERE... NOW, ON THIS MOON. I FELT HIS PRESENCE. I HAVE TO FACE HIM.
WHY?
HE'S MY FATHER.
YOUR FATHER?!
THERE'S MORE. IF I DON'T MAKE IT BACK, YOU'RE THE ONLY HOPE FOR THE ALLIANCE. THE FORCE IS STRONG IN MY FAMILY, LEIA.
MY FATHER HAS IT... I HAVE IT... AND MY SISTER HAS IT.
?
YES. IT'S YOU LEIA.
I KNOW. SOMEHOW... I'VE ALWAYS KNOWN.
THEN YOU KNOW WHY I HAVE TO FACE HIM. BECAUSE... THERE IS GOOD IN HIM.
"I CAN SAVE HIM."

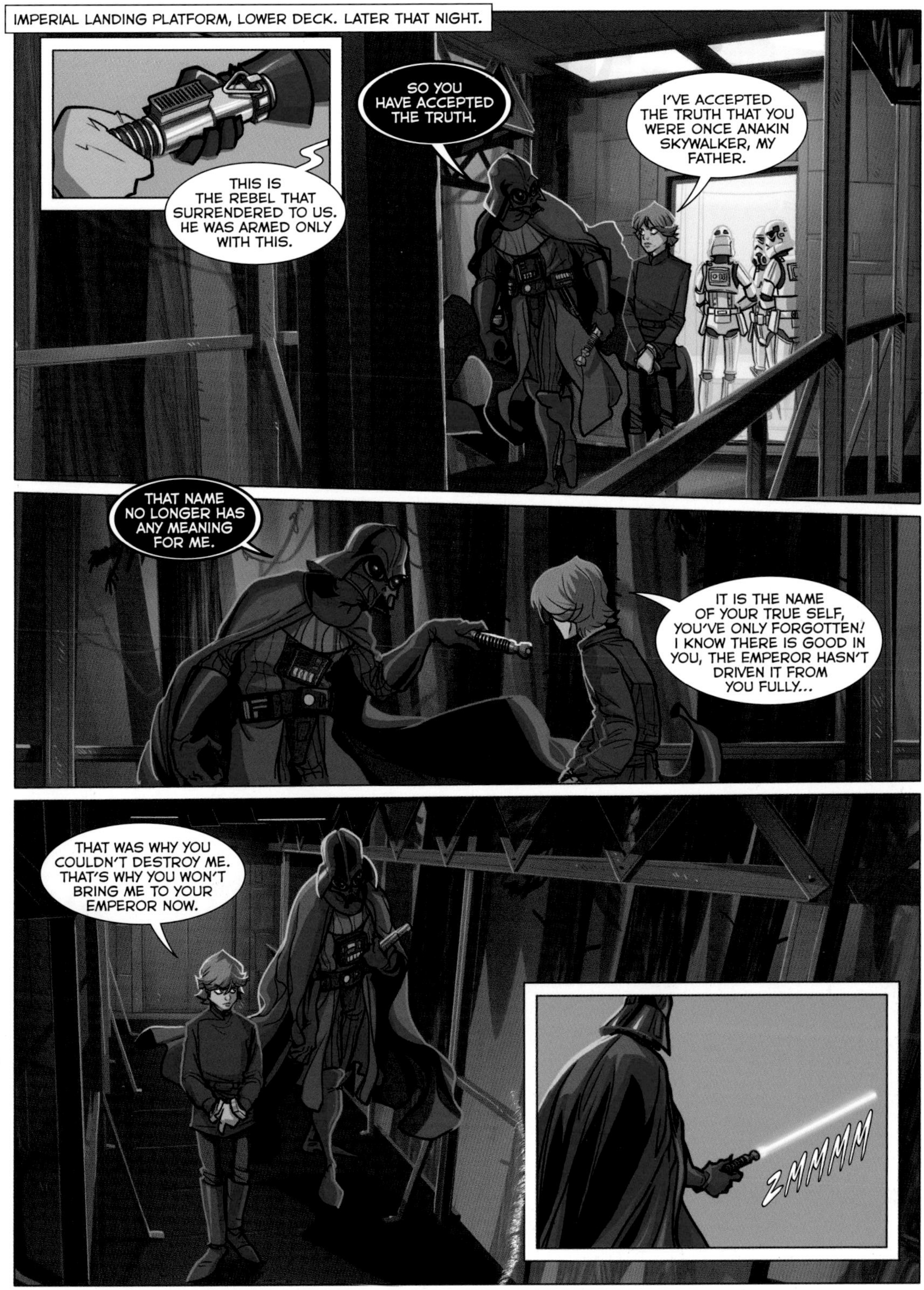
IMPERIAL LANDING PLATFORM, LOWER DECK. LATER THAT NIGHT.
THIS IS THE REBEL THAT SURRENDERED TO US. HE WAS ARMED ONLY WITH THIS.
SO YOU HAVE ACCEPTED THE TRUTH.
I'VE ACCEPTED THE TRUTH THAT YOU WERE ONCE ANAKIN SKYWALKER, MY FATHER.
THAT NAME NO LONGER HAS ANY MEANING FOR ME.
IT IS THE NAME OF YOUR TRUE SELF, YOU'VE ONLY FORGOTTEN! I KNOW THERE IS GOOD IN YOU, THE EMPEROR HASN'T DRIVEN IT FROM YOU FULLY...
THAT WAS WHY YOU COULDN'T DESTROY ME. THAT'S WHY YOU WON'T BRING ME TO YOUR EMPEROR NOW.
ZMMMM

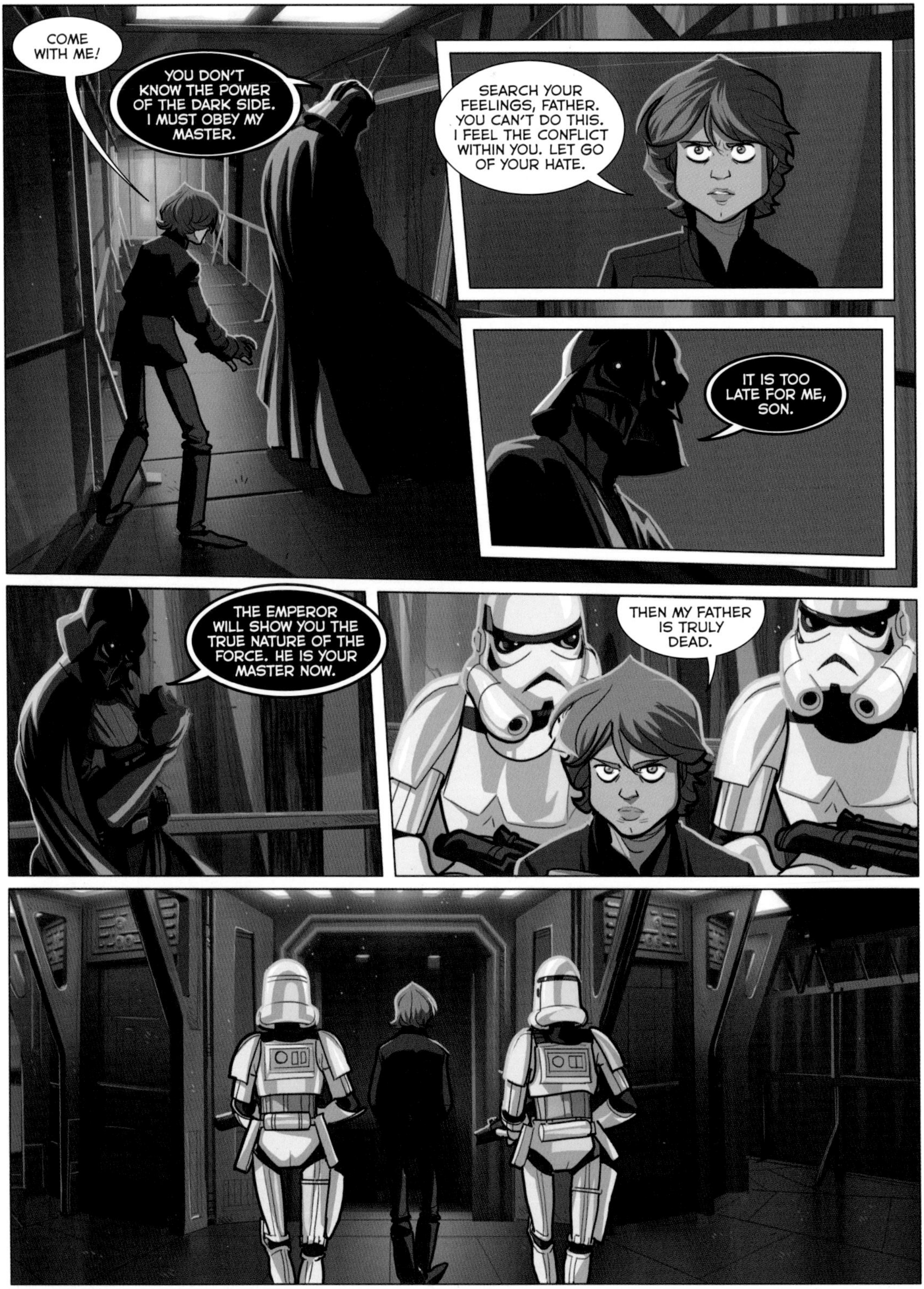
COME WITH ME!
YOU DON'T KNOW THE POWER OF THE DARK SIDE. I MUST OBEY MY MASTER.
SEARCH YOUR FEELINGS, FATHER. YOU CAN'T DO THIS. I FEEL THE CONFLICT WITHIN YOU. LET GO OF YOUR HATE.
IT IS TOO LATE FOR ME, SON.
THE EMPEROR WILL SHOW YOU THE TRUE NATURE OF THE FORCE. HE IS YOUR MASTER NOW.
THEN MY FATHER IS TRULY DEAD.

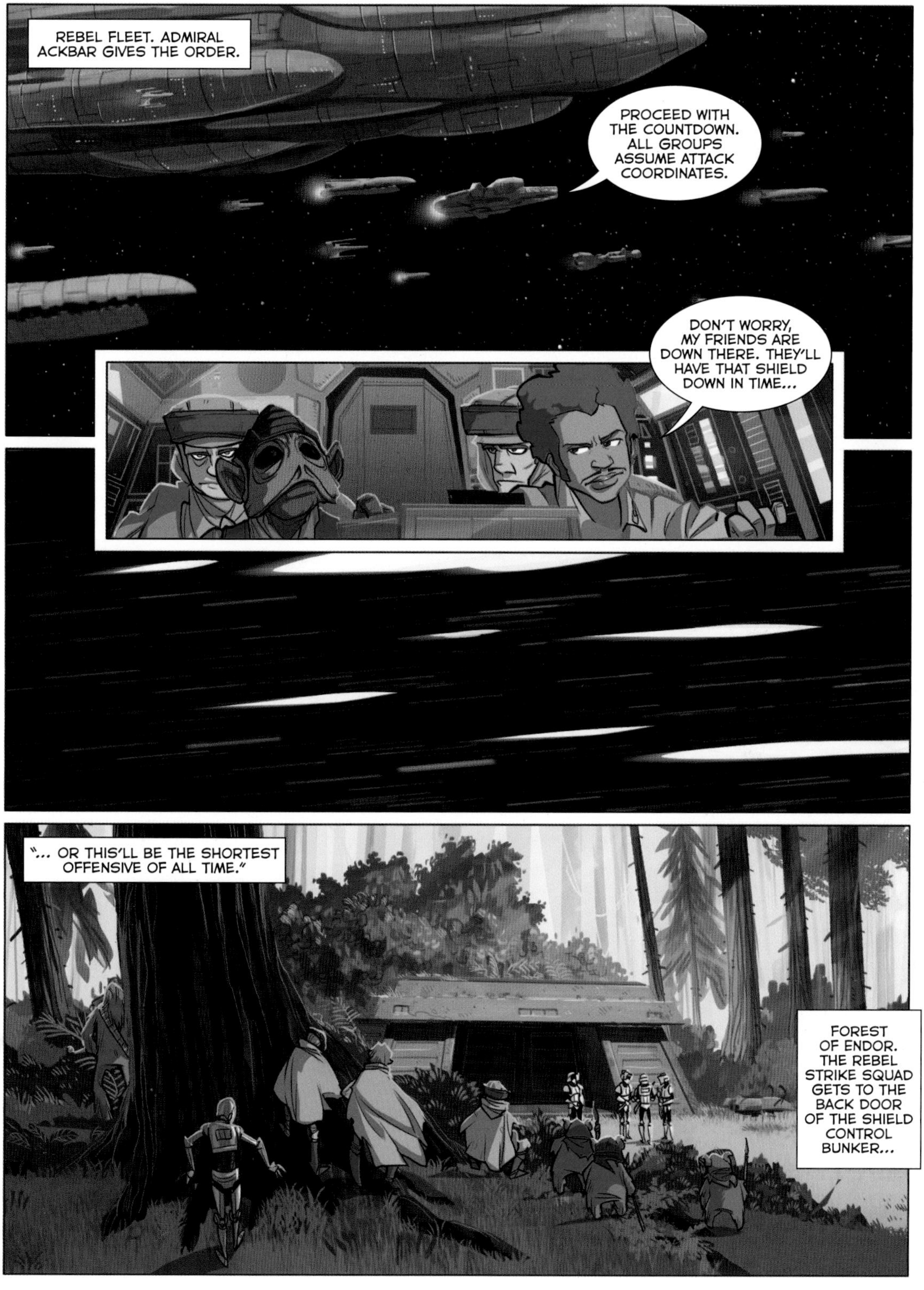
REBEL FLEET. ADMIRAL ACKBAR GIVES THE ORDER.
PROCEED WITH THE COUNTDOWN. ALL GROUPS ASSUME ATTACK COORDINATES.
DON'T WORRY, MY FRIENDS ARE DOWN THERE. THEY'LL HAVE THAT SHIELD DOWN IN TIME...
"... OR THIS'LL BE THE SHORTEST OFFENSIVE OF ALL TIME."
FOREST OF ENDOR. THE REBEL STRIKE SQUAD GETS TO THE BACK DOOR OF THE SHIELD CONTROL BUNKER...

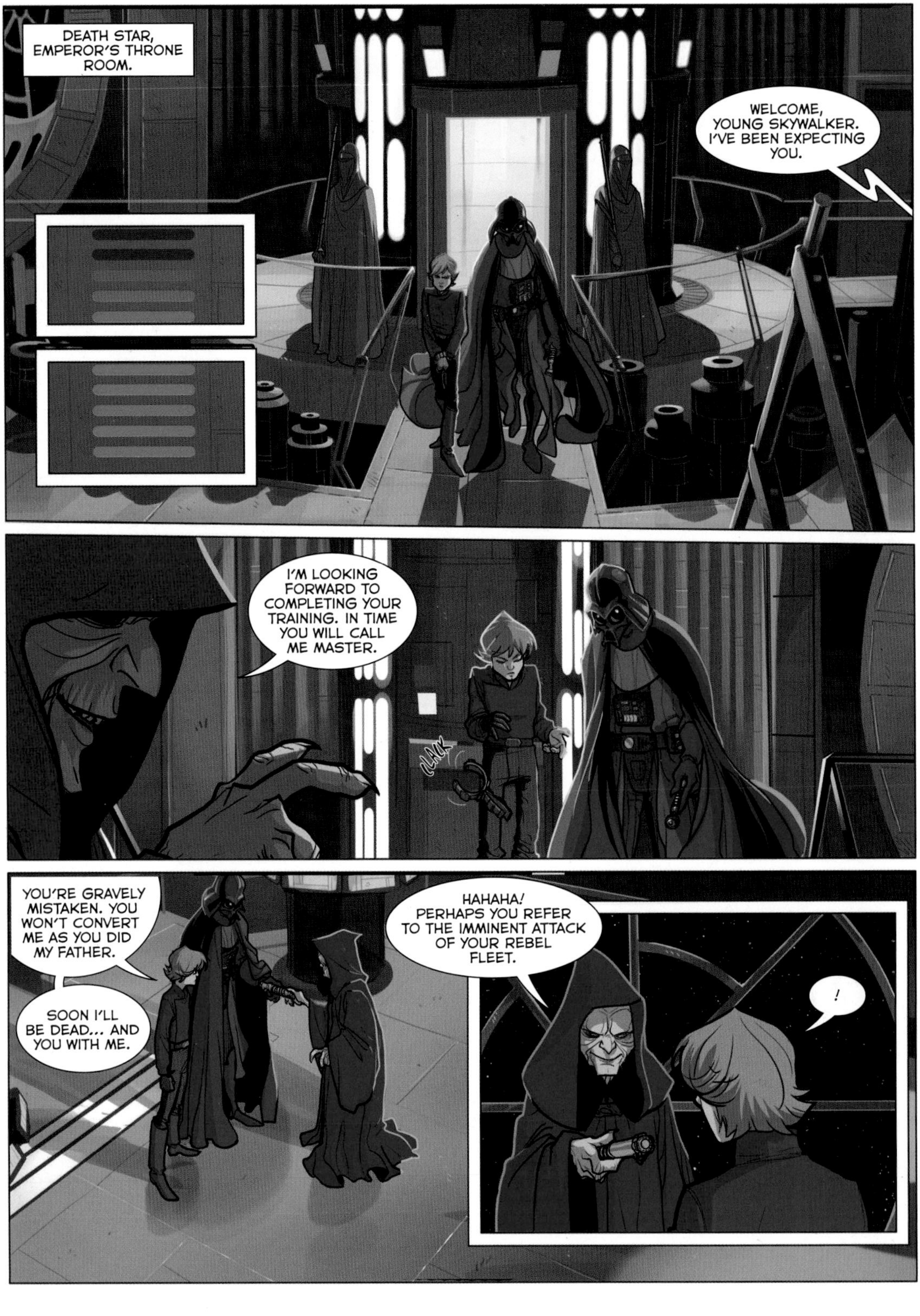
DEATH STAR, EMPEROR'S THRONE ROOM.
WELCOME, YOUNG SKYWALKER. I'VE BEEN EXPECTING YOU.
I'M LOOKING FORWARD TO COMPLETING YOUR TRAINING. IN TIME YOU WILL CALL ME MASTER.
CLACK
YOU'RE GRAVELY MISTAKEN. YOU WON'T CONVERT ME AS YOU DID MY FATHER.
SOON I'LL BE DEAD... AND YOU WITH ME.
HAHAHA! PERHAPS YOU REFER TO THE IMMINENT ATTACK OF YOUR REBEL FLEET.
!

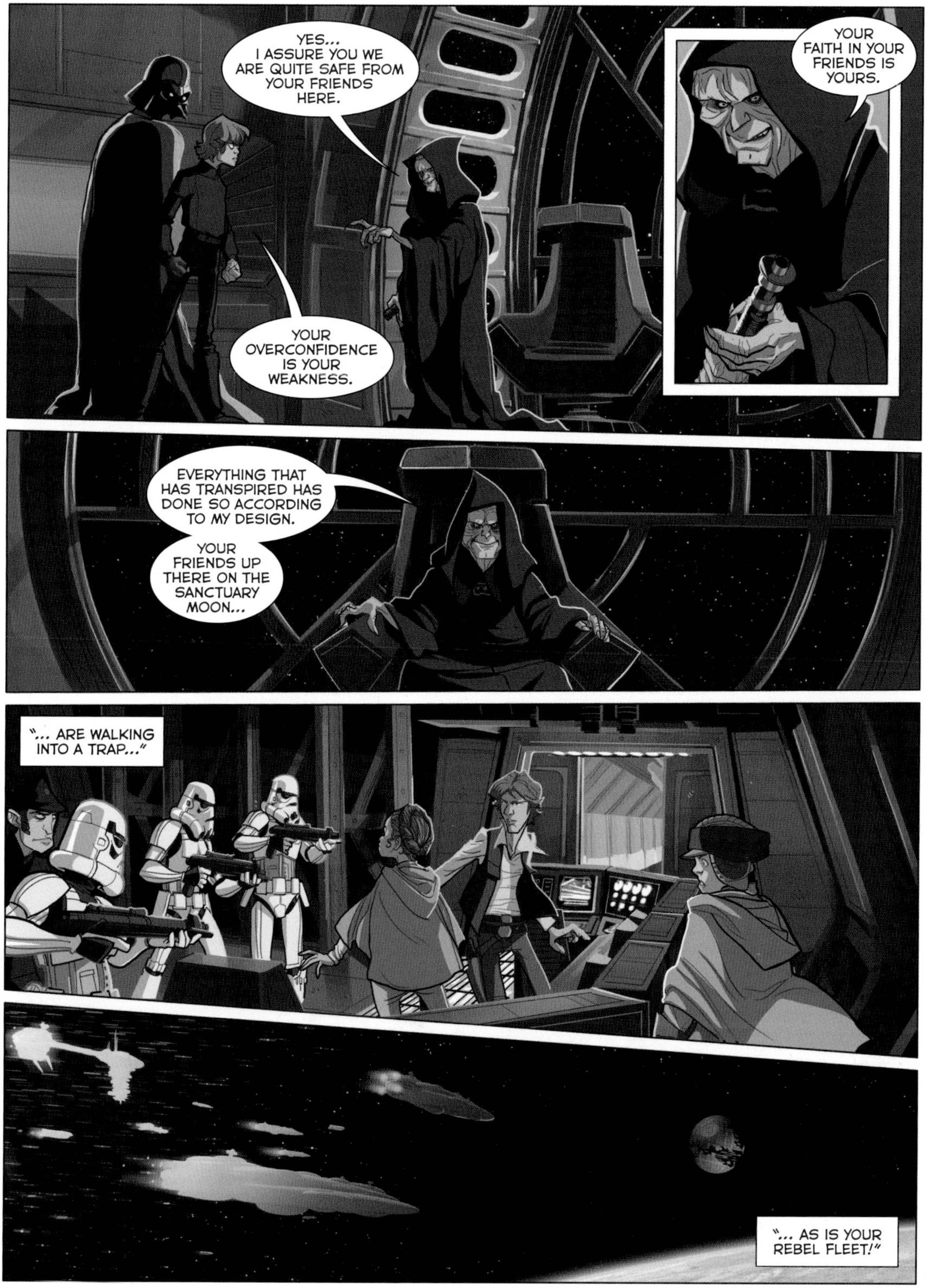
YES... I ASSURE YOU WE ARE QUITE SAFE FROM YOUR FRIENDS HERE.
YOUR OVERCONFIDENCE IS YOUR WEAKNESS.
YOUR FAITH IN YOUR FRIENDS IS YOURS.
EVERYTHING THAT HAS TRANSPIRED HAS DONE SO ACCORDING TO MY DESIGN.
YOUR FRIENDS UP THERE ON THE SANCTUARY MOON...
"... ARE WALKING INTO A TRAP..."
"... AS IS YOUR REBEL FLEET!"

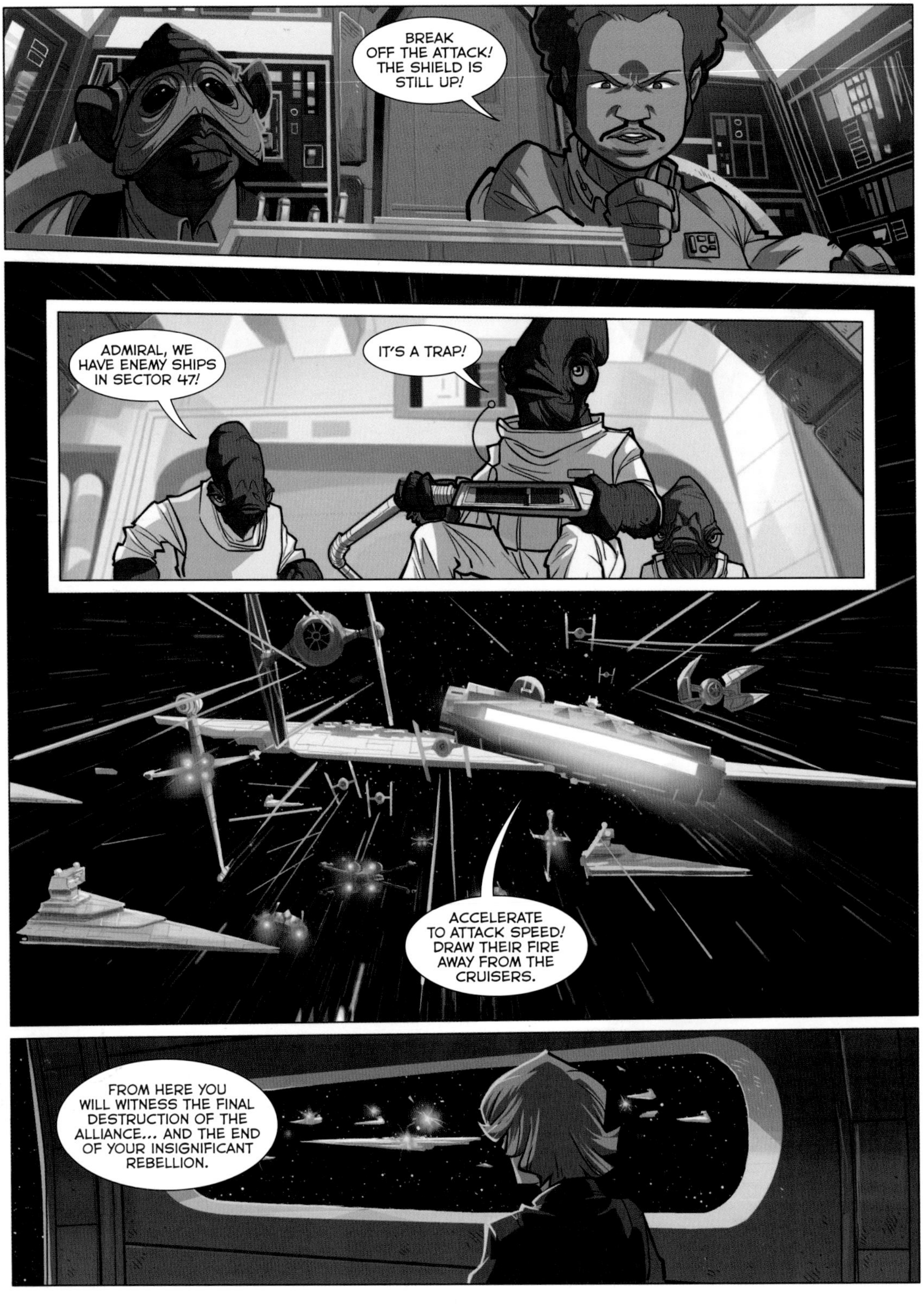
BREAK OFF THE ATTACK! THE SHIELD IS STILL UP!
ADMIRAL, WE HAVE ENEMY SHIPS IN SECTOR 47!
IT'S A TRAP!
ACCELERATE TO ATTACK SPEED! DRAW THEIR FIRE AWAY FROM THE CRUISERS.
FROM HERE YOU WILL WITNESS THE FINAL DESTRUCTION OF THE ALLIANCE... AND THE END OF YOUR INSIGNIFICANT REBELLION.

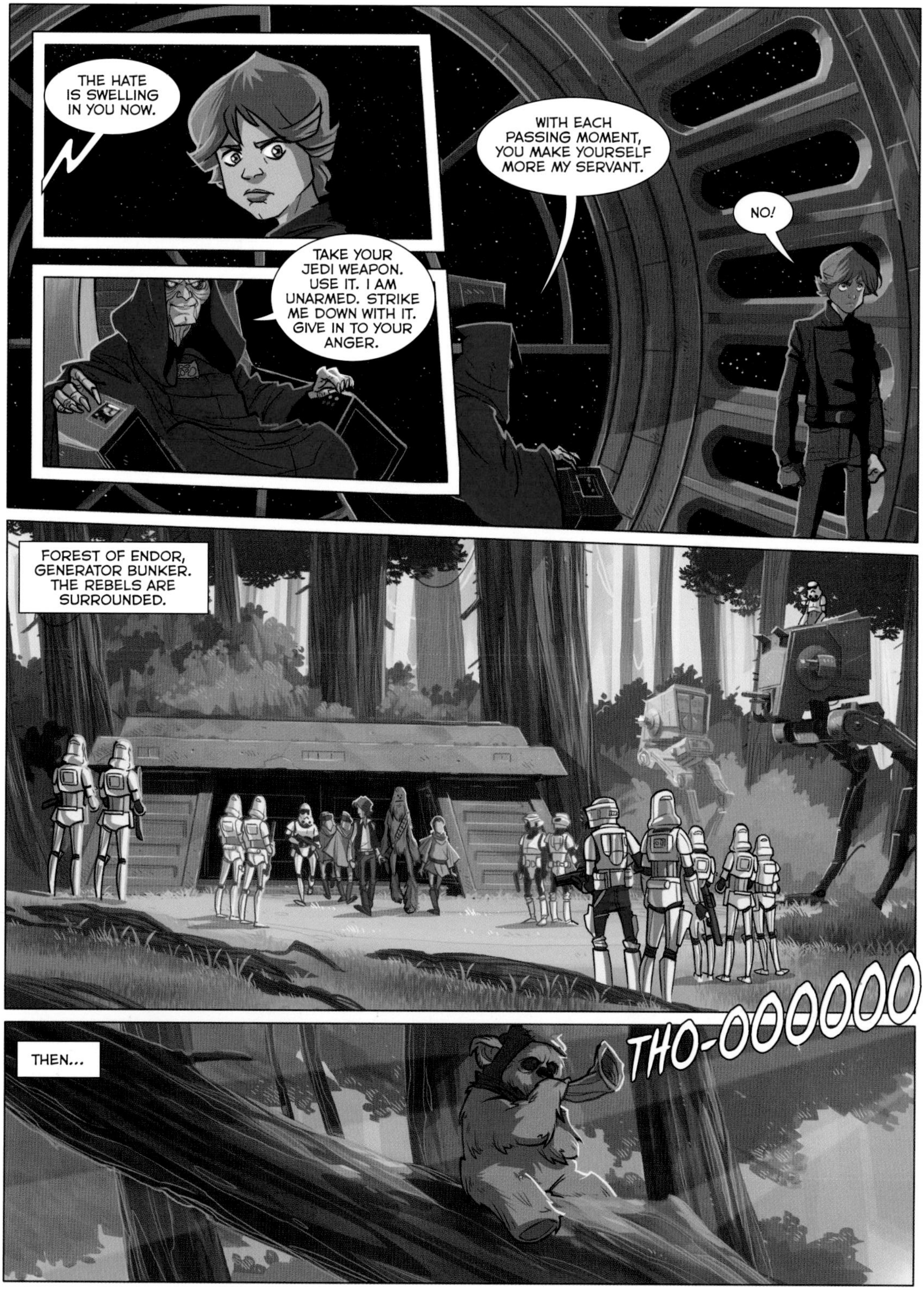
THE HATE IS SWELLING IN YOU NOW.
TAKE YOUR JEDI WEAPON. USE IT. I AM UNARMED. STRIKE ME DOWN WITH IT. GIVE IN TO YOUR ANGER.
WITH EACH PASSING MOMENT, YOU MAKE YOURSELF MORE MY SERVANT.
NO!
FOREST OF ENDOR, GENERATOR BUNKER. THE REBELS ARE SURROUNDED.
THEN...
THO-OOOOOO

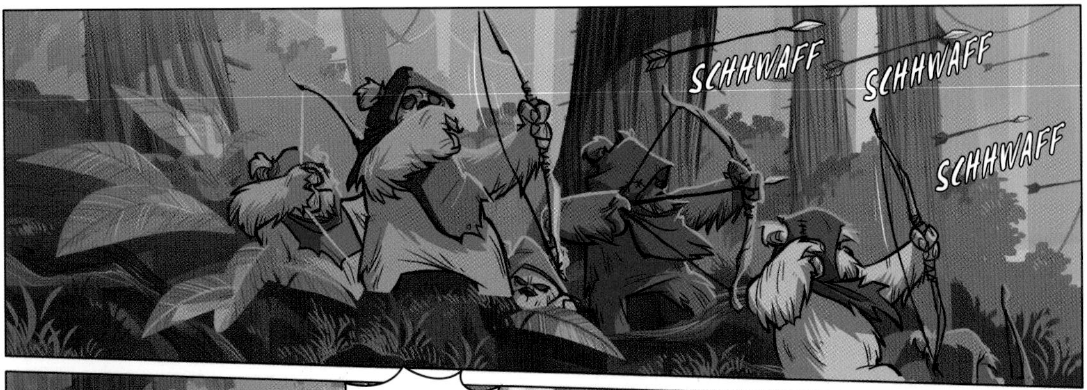
SCHHWAFF
SCHHWAFF
SCHHWAFF

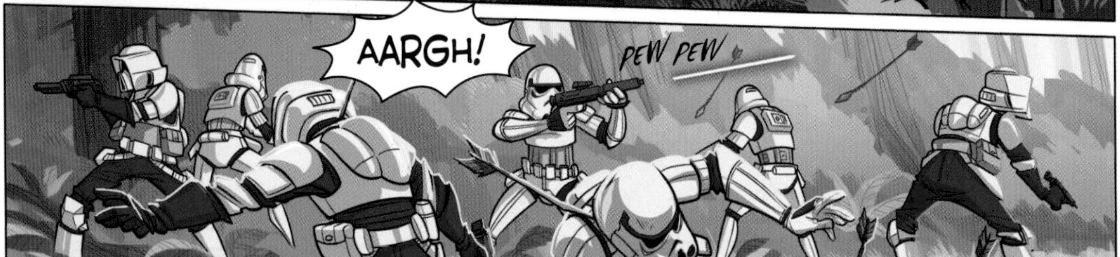
AARGH!
PEW PEW

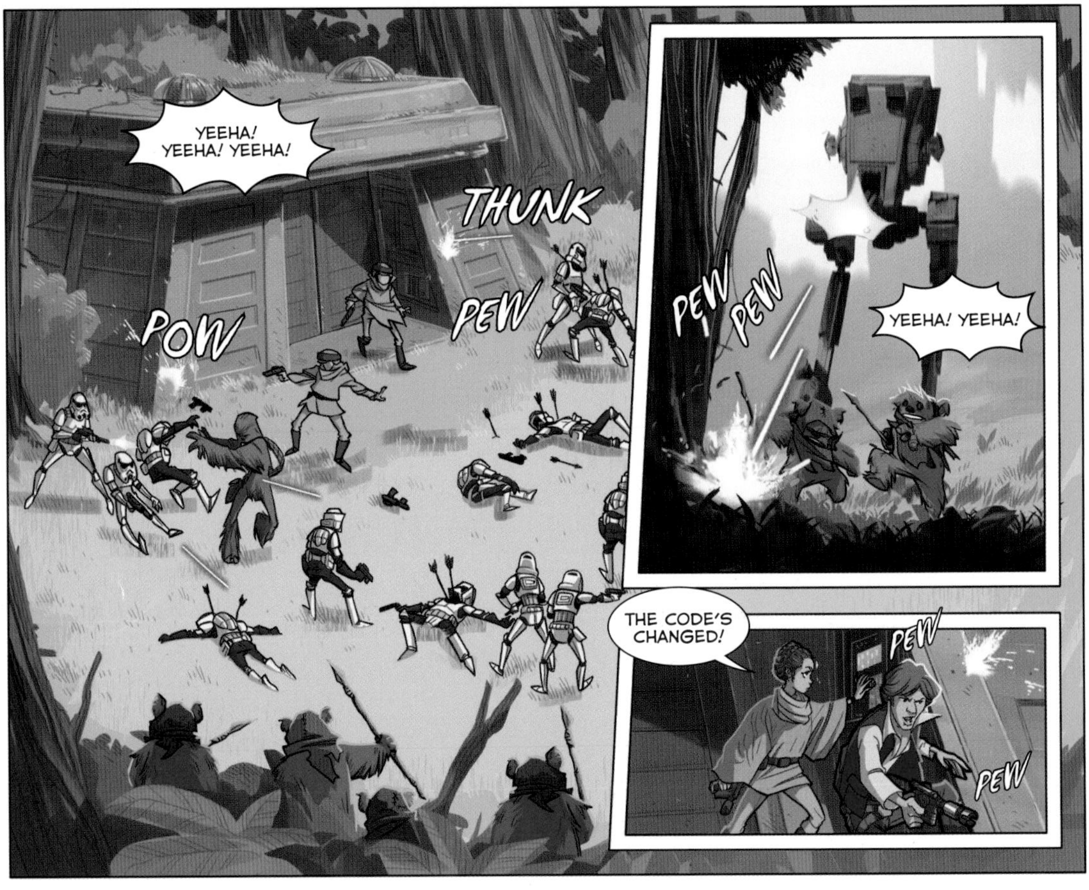
YEEHA! YEEHA! YEEHA!
THUNK
POW
PEW
PEW
PEW
YEEHA! YEEHA!
THE CODE'S CHANGED!
PEW
PEW

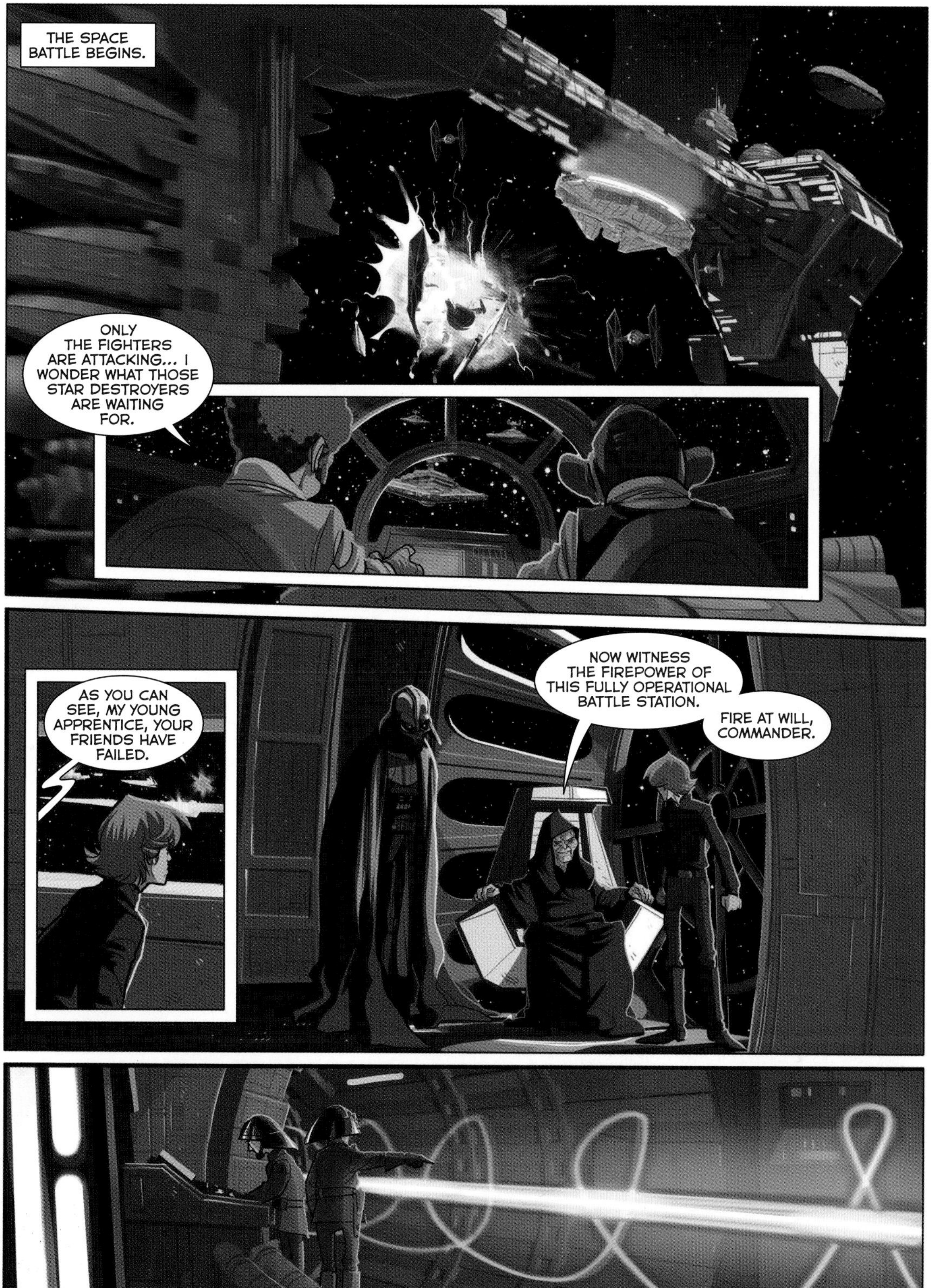
THE SPACE BATTLE BEGINS.
ONLY THE FIGHTERS ARE ATTACKING... I WONDER WHAT THOSE STAR DESTROYERS ARE WAITING FOR.
AS YOU CAN SEE, MY YOUNG APPRENTICE, YOUR FRIENDS HAVE FAILED.
NOW WITNESS THE FIREPOWER OF THIS FULLY OPERATIONAL BATTLE STATION.
FIRE AT WILL, COMMANDER.

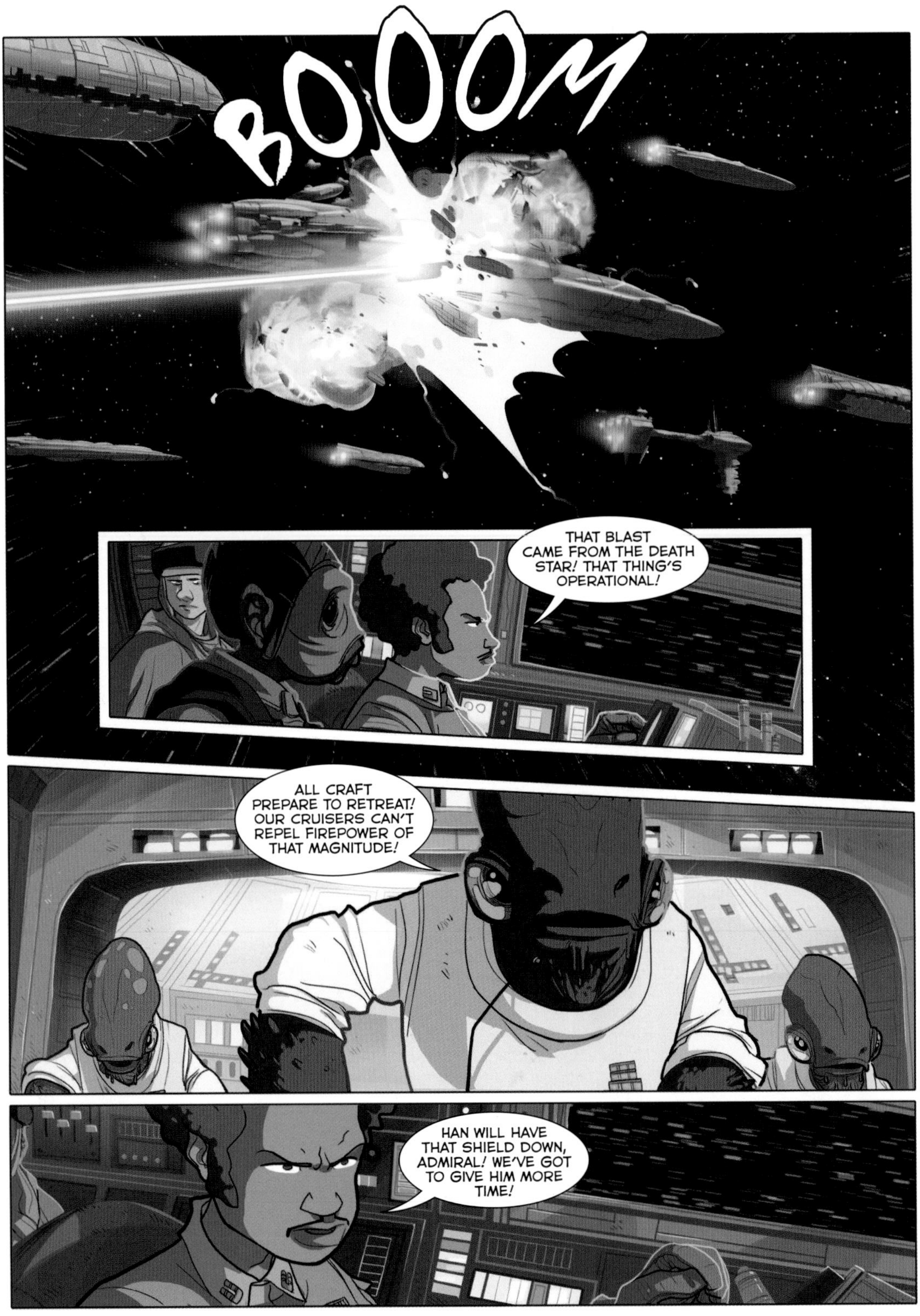
BOOOOM
THAT BLAST CAME FROM THE DEATH STAR! THAT THING'S OPERATIONAL!
ALL CRAFT PREPARE TO RETREAT! OUR CRUISERS CAN'T REPEL FIREPOWER OF THAT MAGNITUDE!
HAN WILL HAVE THAT SHIELD DOWN, ADMIRAL! WE'VE GOT TO GIVE HIM MORE TIME!

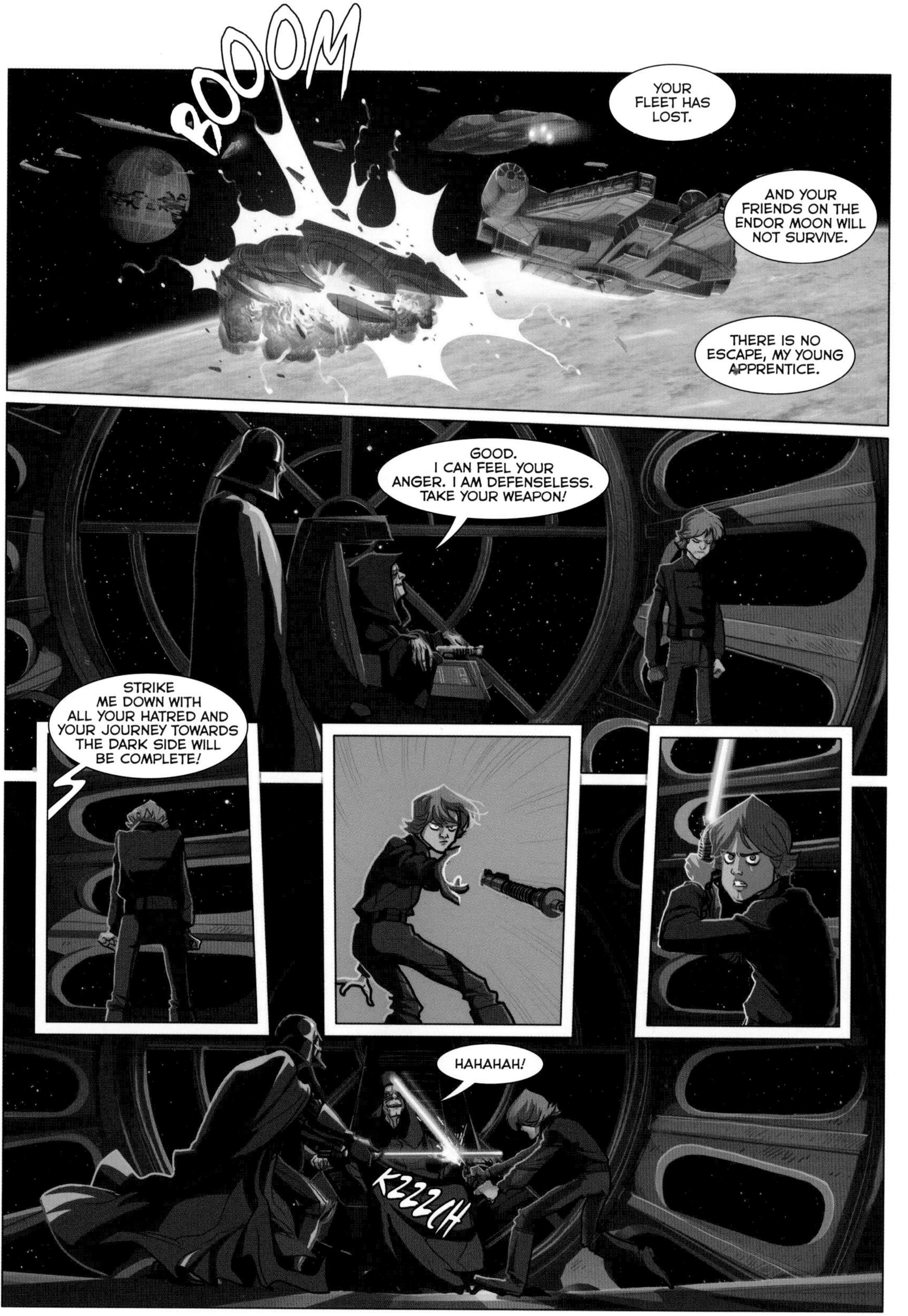
BOOOM
YOUR FLEET HAS LOST.
AND YOUR FRIENDS ON THE ENDOR MOON WILL NOT SURVIVE.
THERE IS NO ESCAPE, MY YOUNG APPRENTICE.
GOOD. I CAN FEEL YOUR ANGER. I AM DEFENSELESS. TAKE YOUR WEAPON!
STRIKE ME DOWN WITH ALL YOUR HATRED AND YOUR JOURNEY TOWARDS THE DARK SIDE WILL BE COMPLETE!
HAHAHAH!
KZZZCH

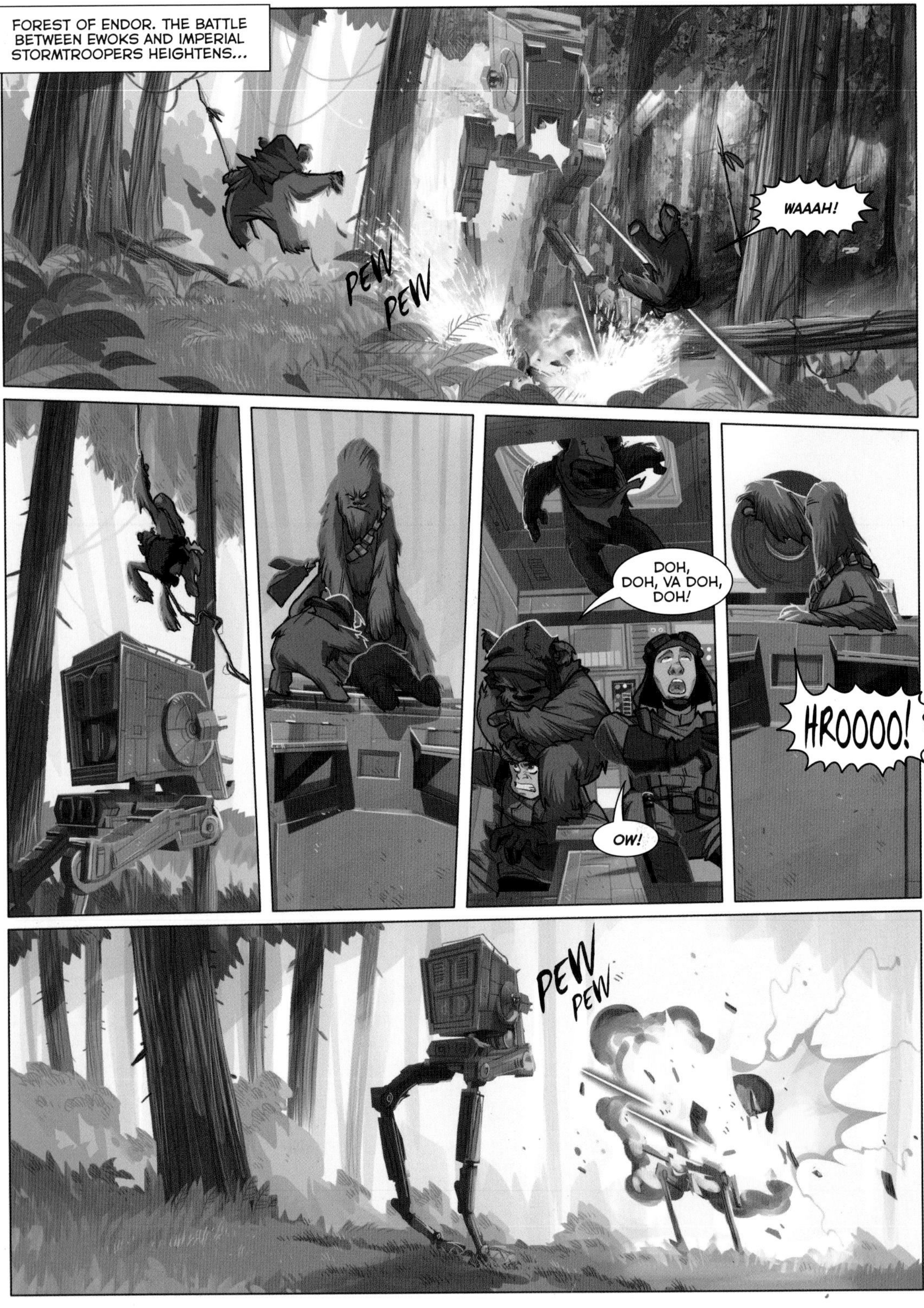
FOREST OF ENDOR. THE BATTLE BETWEEN EWOKS AND IMPERIAL STORMTROOPERS HEIGHTENS...
PEW
PEW
WAAAH!
DOH, DOH, VA DOH, DOH!
OW!
HROOOO!
PEW
PEW

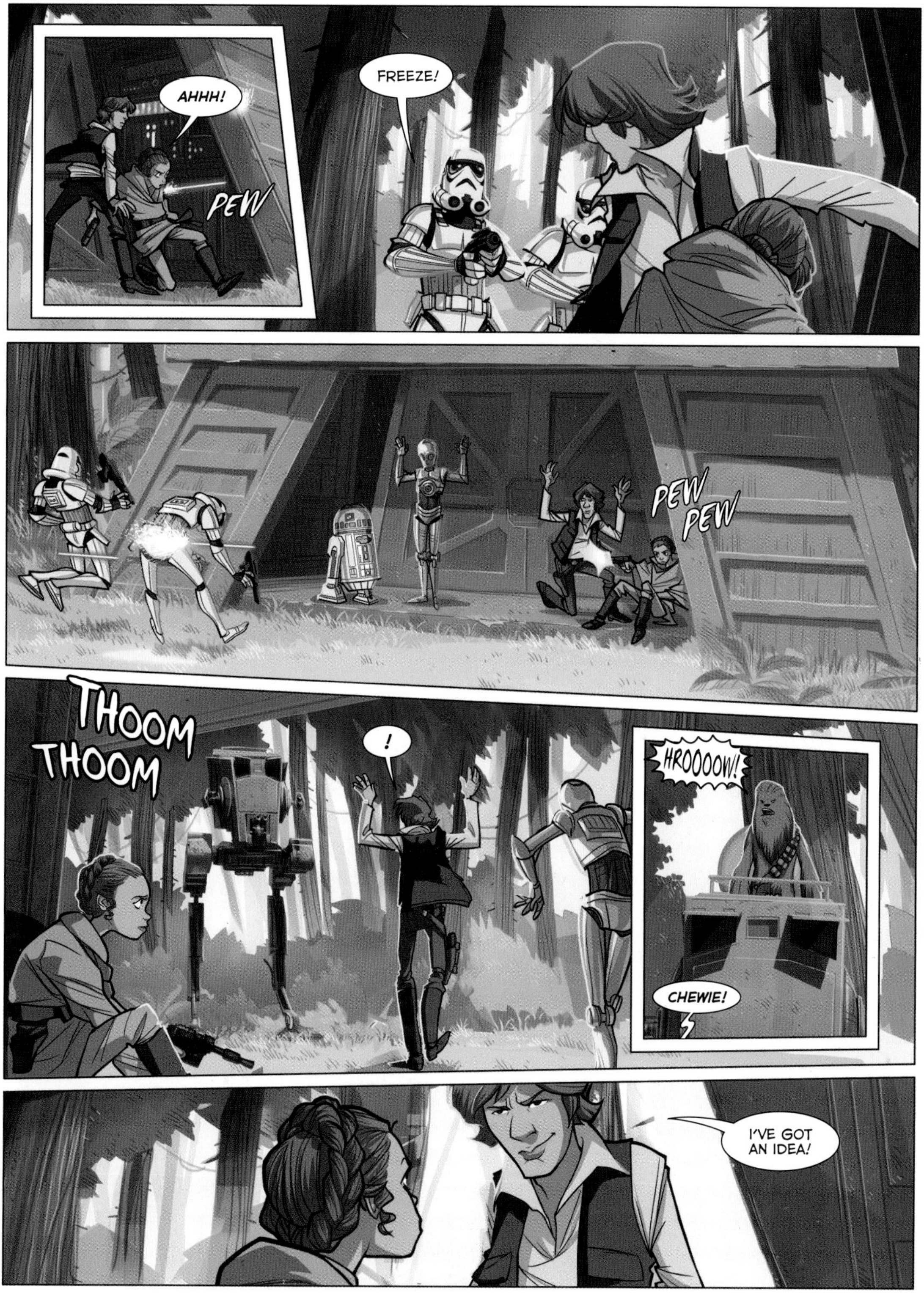
AHHH!
PEW
FREEZE!
PEW
PEW
THOOM
THOOM
!
HROOOW!
CHEWIE!
I'VE GOT AN IDEA!

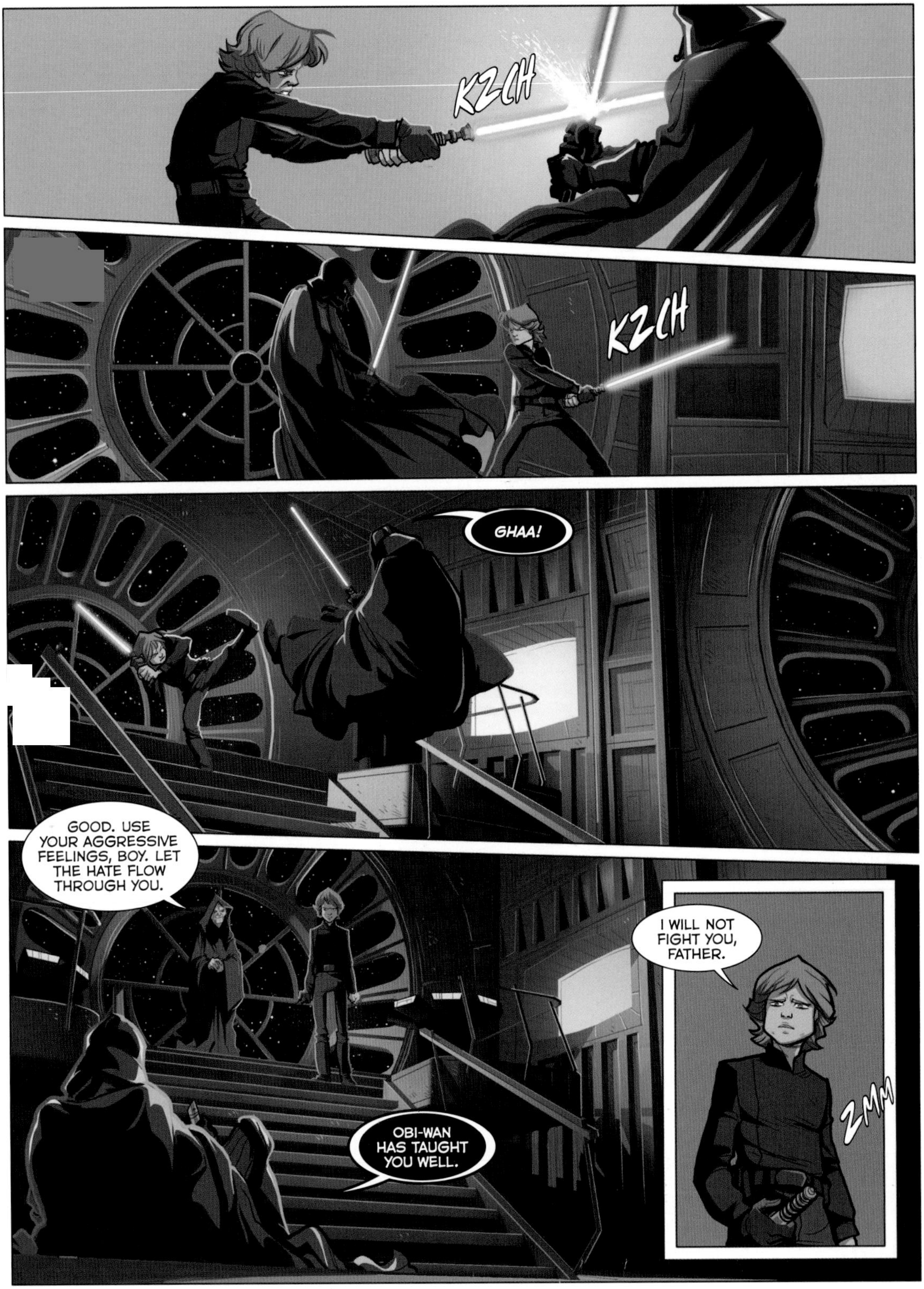
KZCH
KZCH
GHAA!
GOOD. USE YOUR AGGRESSIVE FEELINGS, BOY. LET THE HATE FLOW THROUGH YOU.
OBI-WAN HAS TAUGHT YOU WELL.
I WILL NOT FIGHT YOU, FATHER.
ZMM

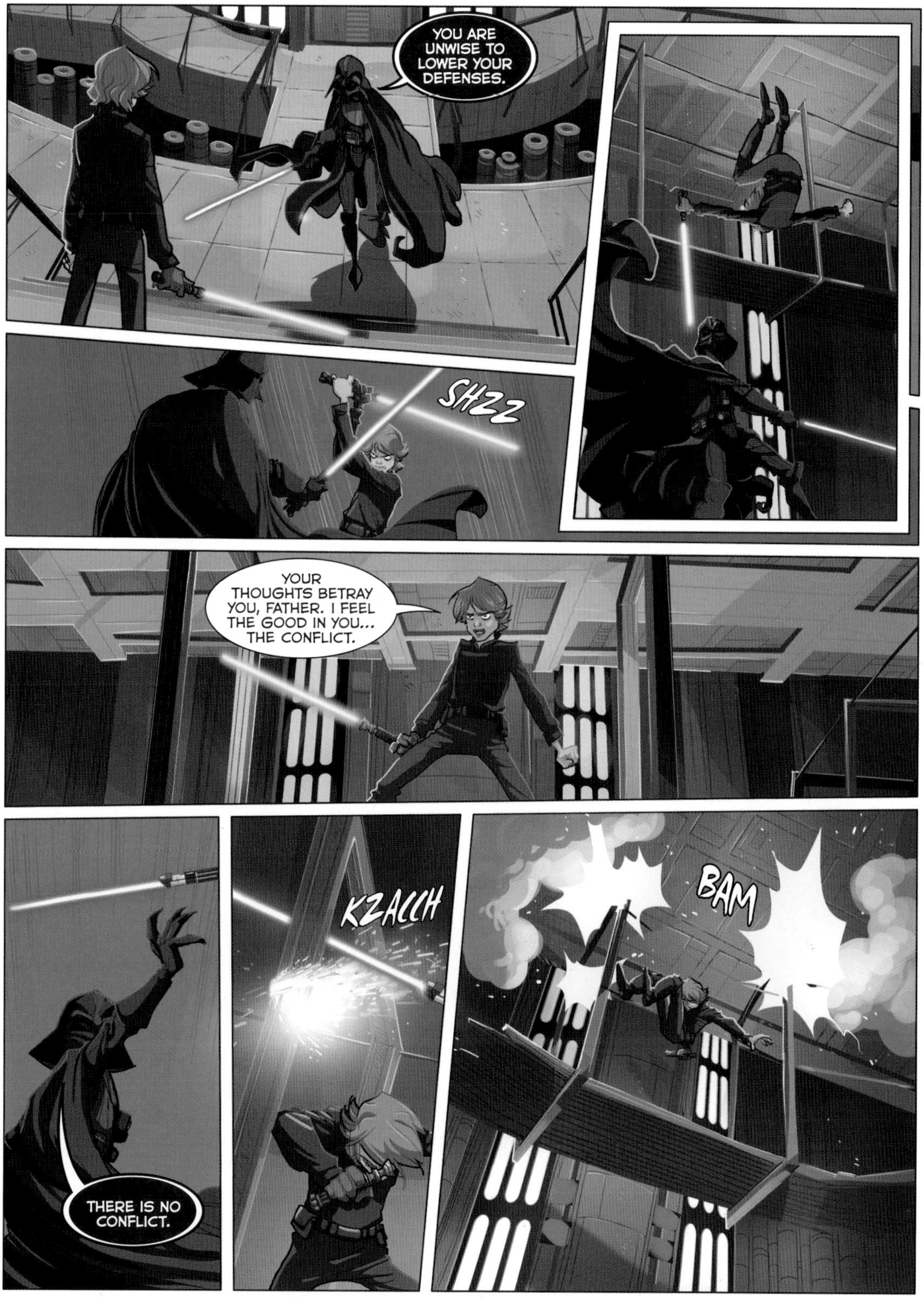

YOU ARE UNWISE TO LOWER YOUR DEFENSES.
SHZZ
YOUR THOUGHTS BETRAY YOU, FATHER. I FEEL THE GOOD IN YOU... THE CONFLICT.
THERE IS NO CONFLICT.
KZACCH
BAM

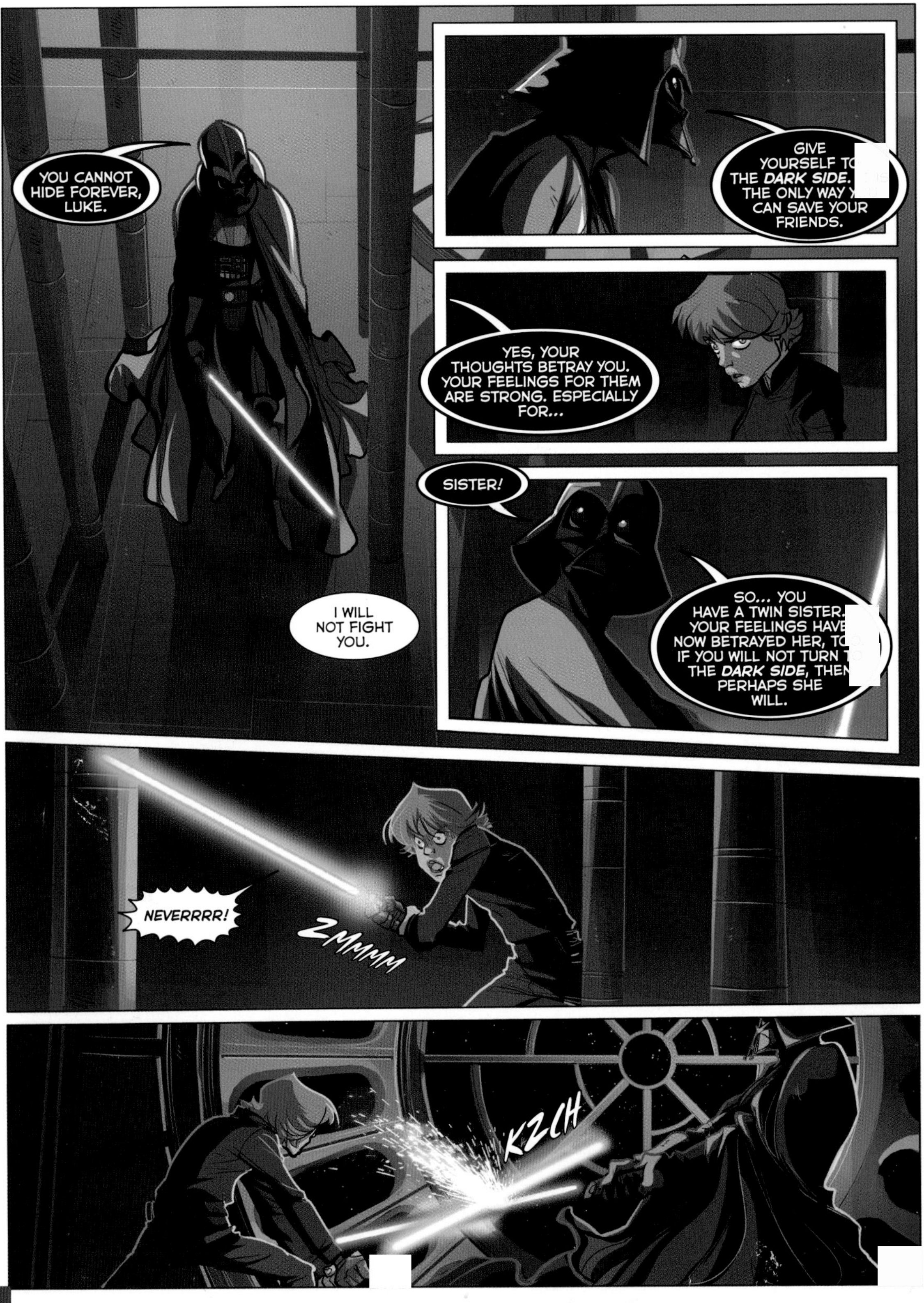

YOU CANNOT HIDE FOREVER, LUKE.
GIVE YOURSELF TO THE *DARK SIDE.* THE ONLY WAY Y CAN SAVE YOUR FRIENDS.
YES, YOUR THOUGHTS BETRAY YOU. YOUR FEELINGS FOR THEM ARE STRONG. ESPECIALLY FOR...
SISTER!
I WILL NOT FIGHT YOU.
SO... YOU HAVE A TWIN SISTER. YOUR FEELINGS HAVE NOW BETRAYED HER, TO IF YOU WILL NOT TURN T THE *DARK SIDE*, THEN PERHAPS SHE WILL.
NEVERRRR!
ZMMMMM
KZCH

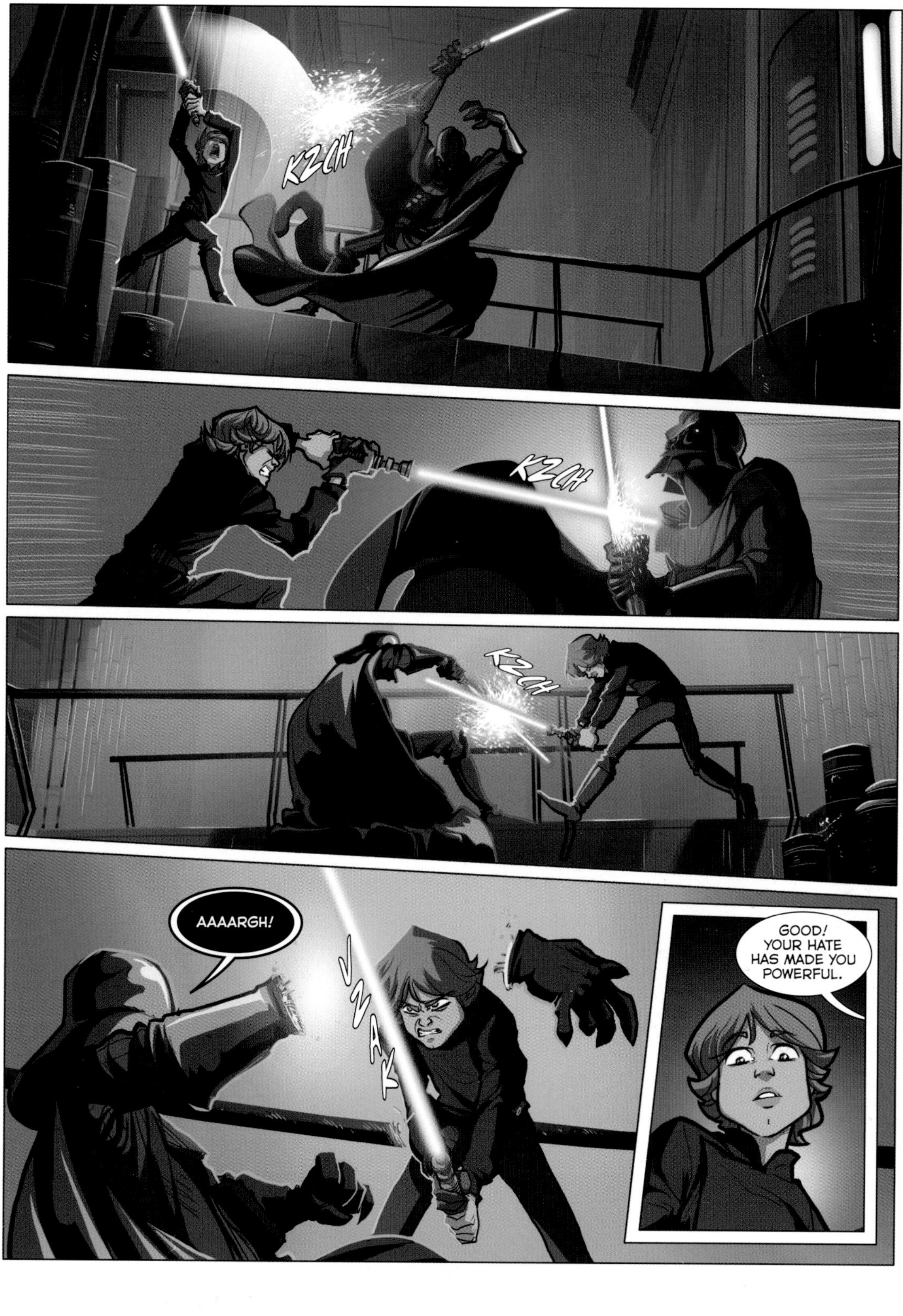
KZCH
KZCH
KZCH
AAAARGH!
VNAK
GOOD! YOUR HATE HAS MADE YOU POWERFUL.

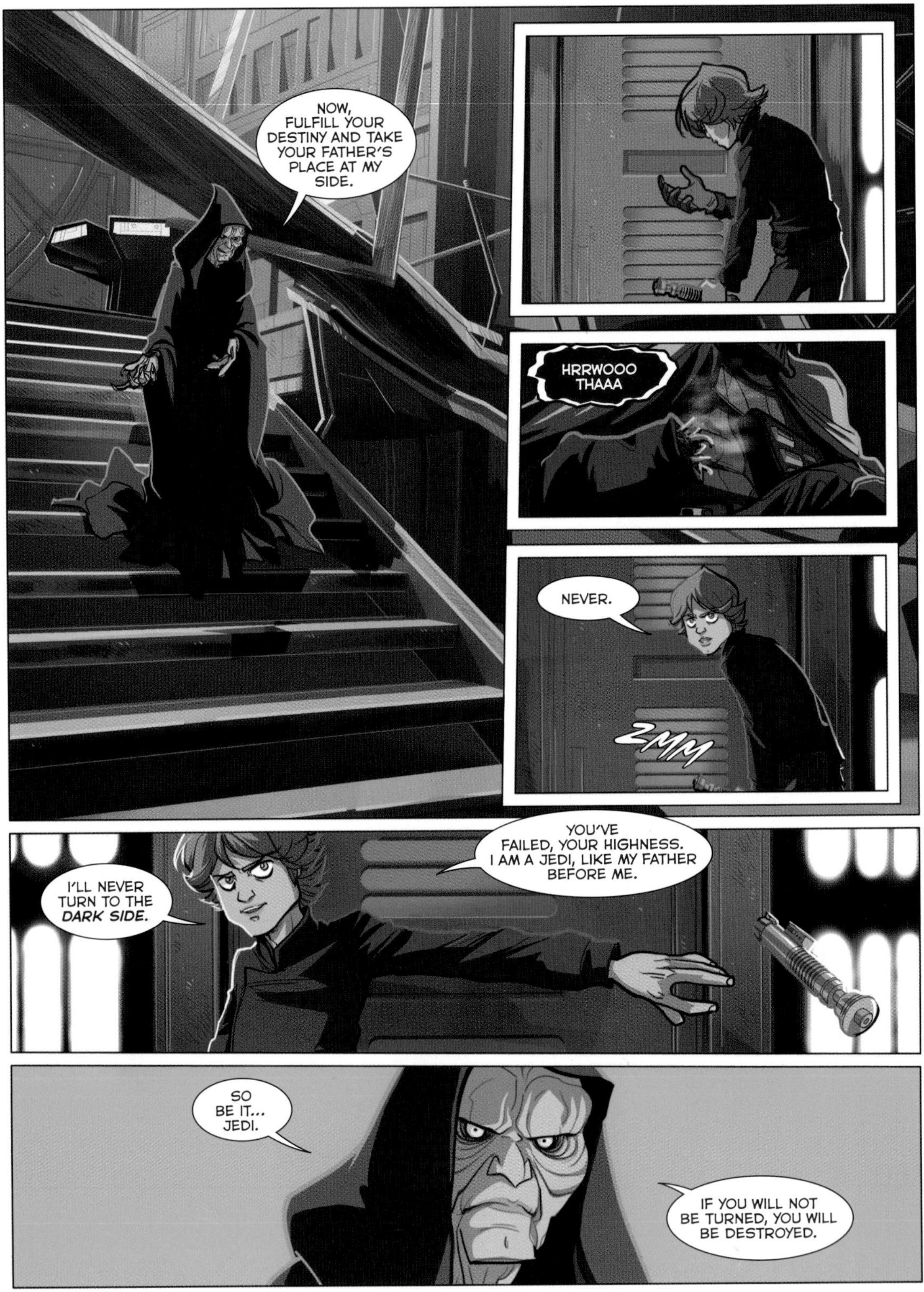
NOW, FULFILL YOUR DESTINY AND TAKE YOUR FATHER'S PLACE AT MY SIDE.
HRRWOOO THAAA
NEVER.
ZMM
I'LL NEVER TURN TO THE *DARK SIDE*.
YOU'VE FAILED, YOUR HIGHNESS. I AM A JEDI, LIKE MY FATHER BEFORE ME.
SO BE IT... JEDI.
IF YOU WILL NOT BE TURNED, YOU WILL BE DESTROYED.

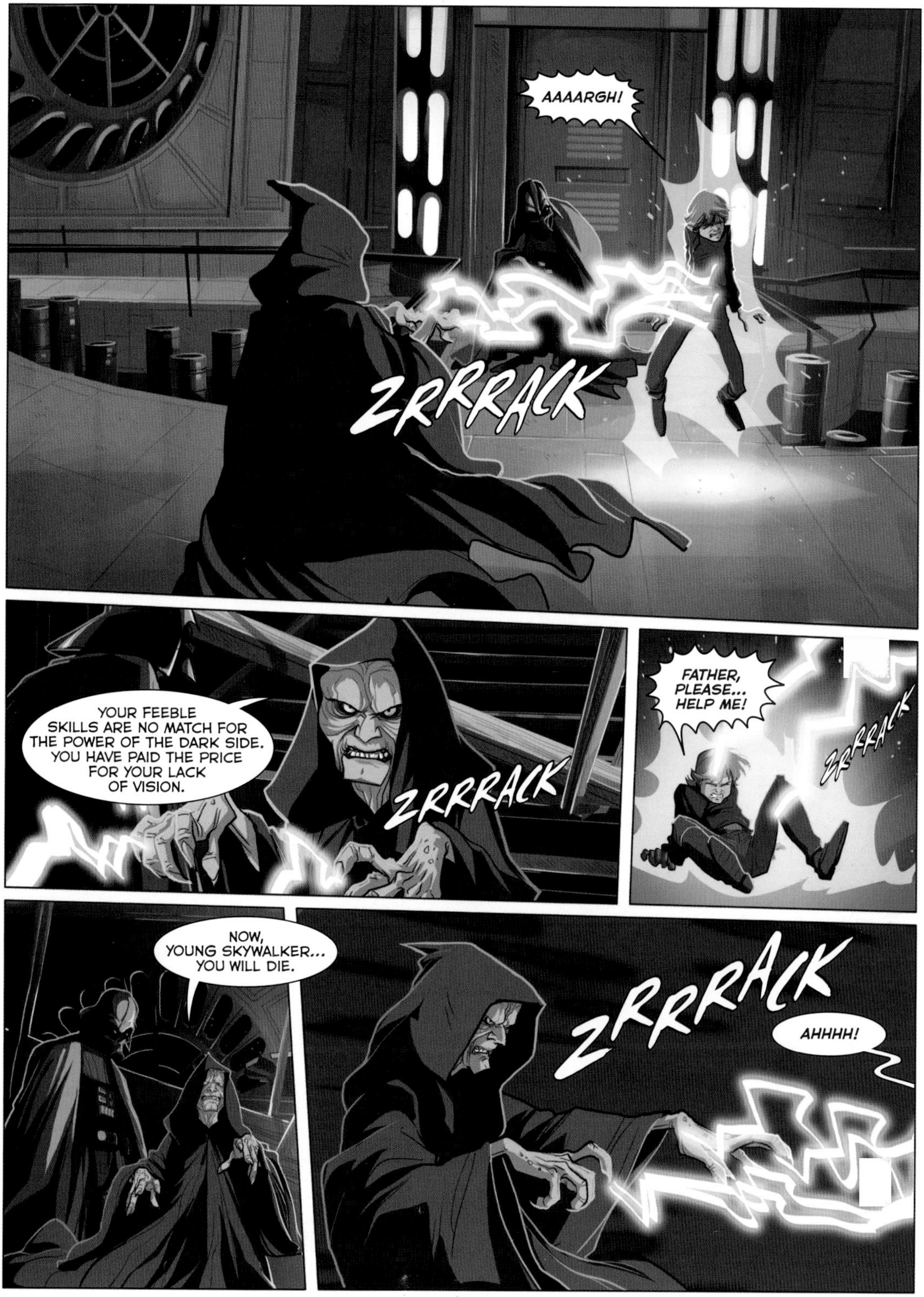
AAAARGH!
ZRRRACK
YOUR FEEBLE SKILLS ARE NO MATCH FOR THE POWER OF THE DARK SIDE. YOU HAVE PAID THE PRICE FOR YOUR LACK OF VISION.
ZRRRACK
FATHER, PLEASE... HELP ME!
ZRRRACK
NOW, YOUNG SKYWALKER... YOU WILL DIE.
ZRRRACK
AHHHH!

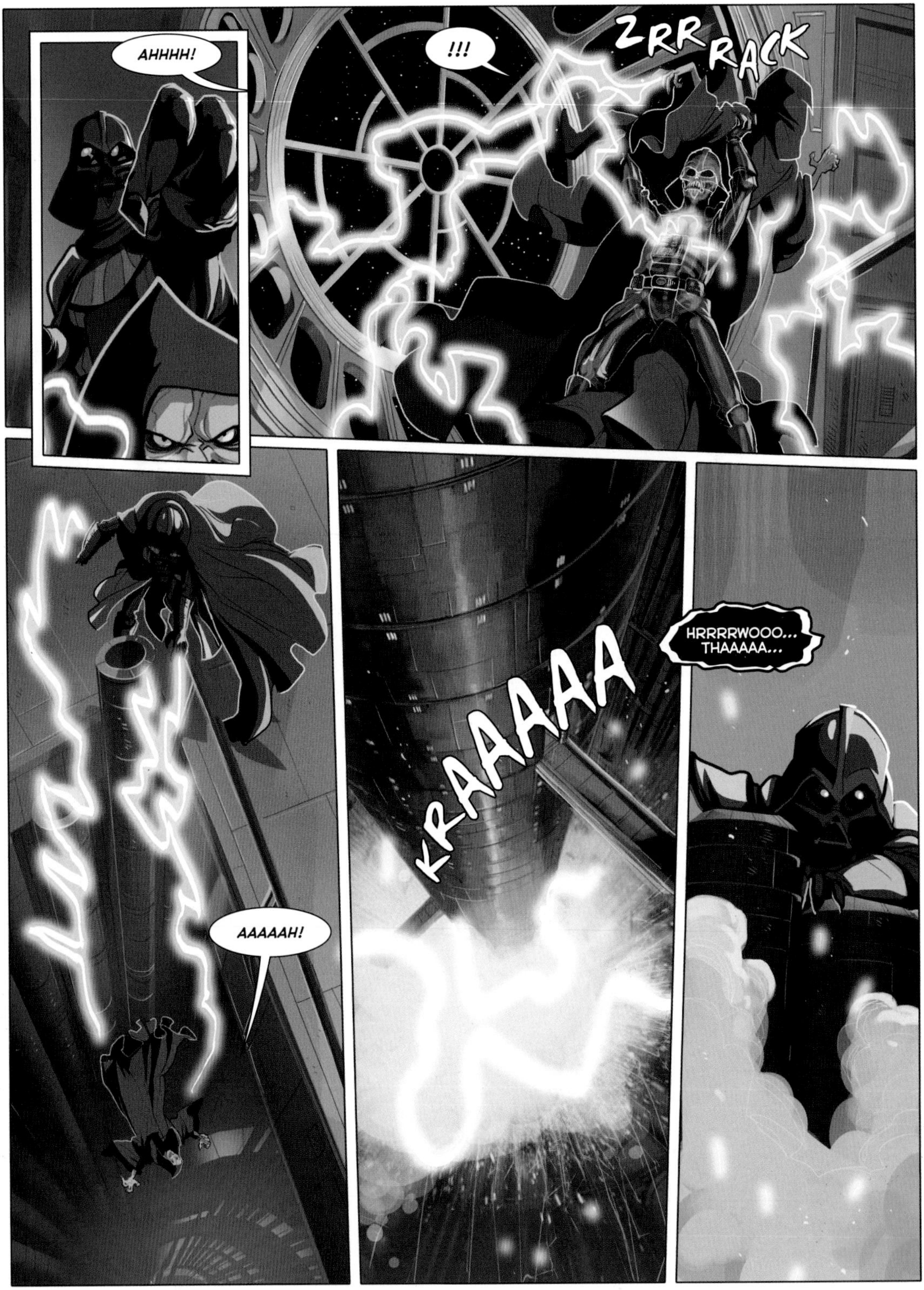
AHHHH!
!!!
ZRR RACK
AAAAAH!
KRAAAAAA
HRRRRWOOO... THAAAAA...

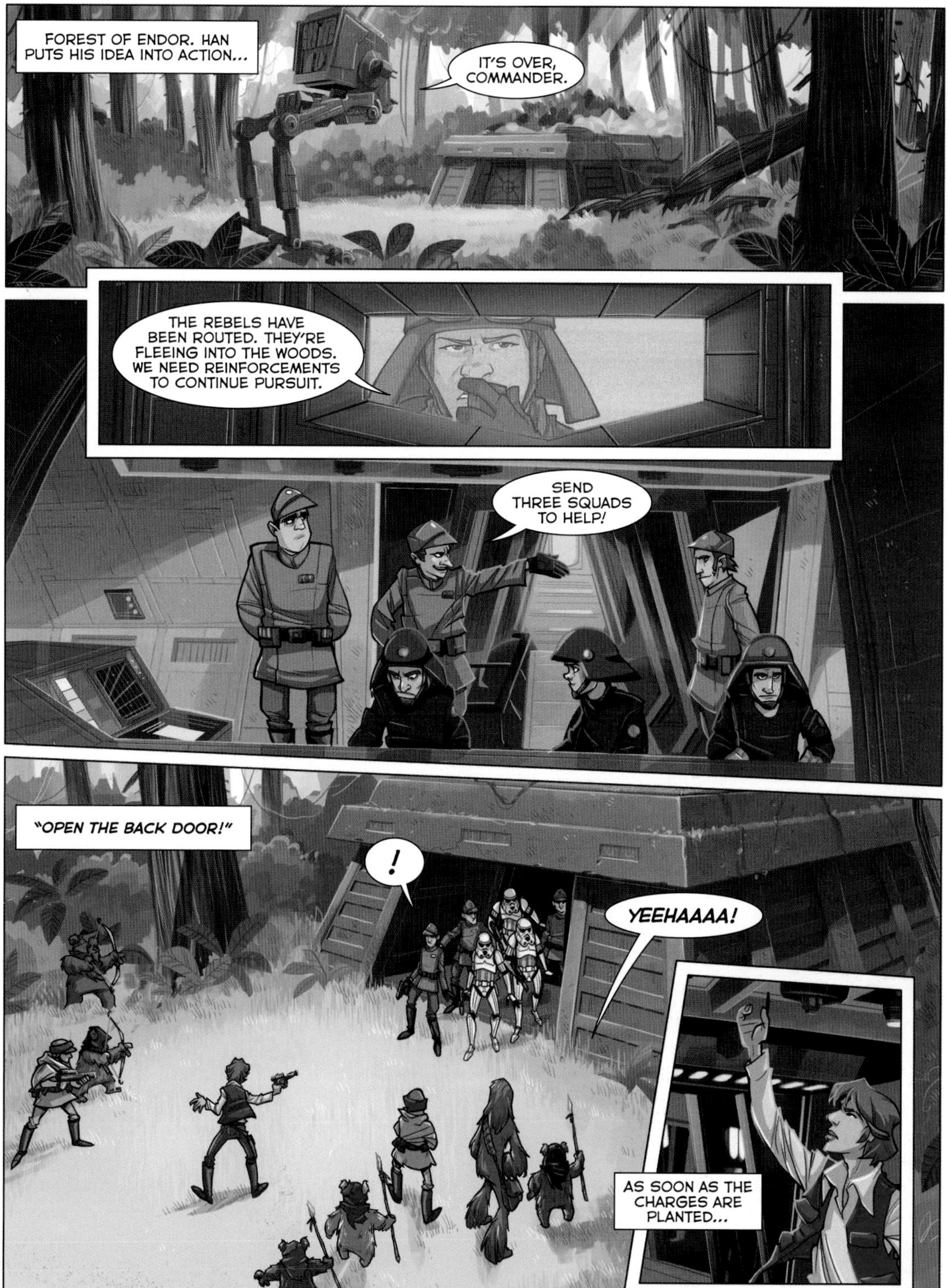
FOREST OF ENDOR. HAN PUTS HIS IDEA INTO ACTION...
IT'S OVER, COMMANDER.
THE REBELS HAVE BEEN ROUTED. THEY'RE FLEEING INTO THE WOODS. WE NEED REINFORCEMENTS TO CONTINUE PURSUIT.
SEND THREE SQUADS TO HELP!
"OPEN THE BACK DOOR!"
!
YEEHAAAA!
AS SOON AS THE CHARGES ARE PLANTED...

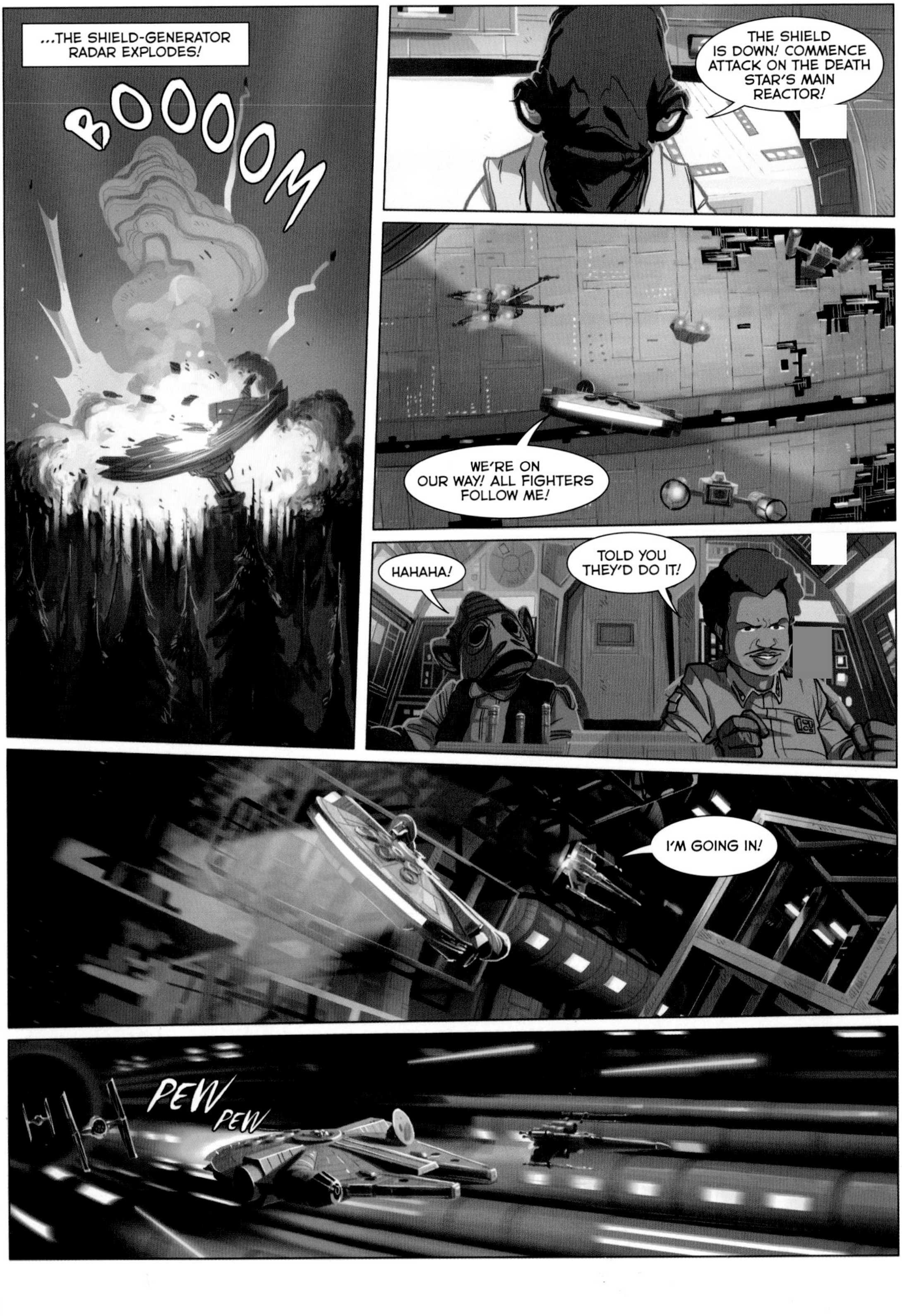
...THE SHIELD-GENERATOR RADAR EXPLODES!
BOOOOM
THE SHIELD IS DOWN! COMMENCE ATTACK ON THE DEATH STAR'S MAIN REACTOR!
WE'RE ON OUR WAY! ALL FIGHTERS FOLLOW ME!
HAHAHA!
TOLD YOU THEY'D DO IT!
I'M GOING IN!
PEW PEW

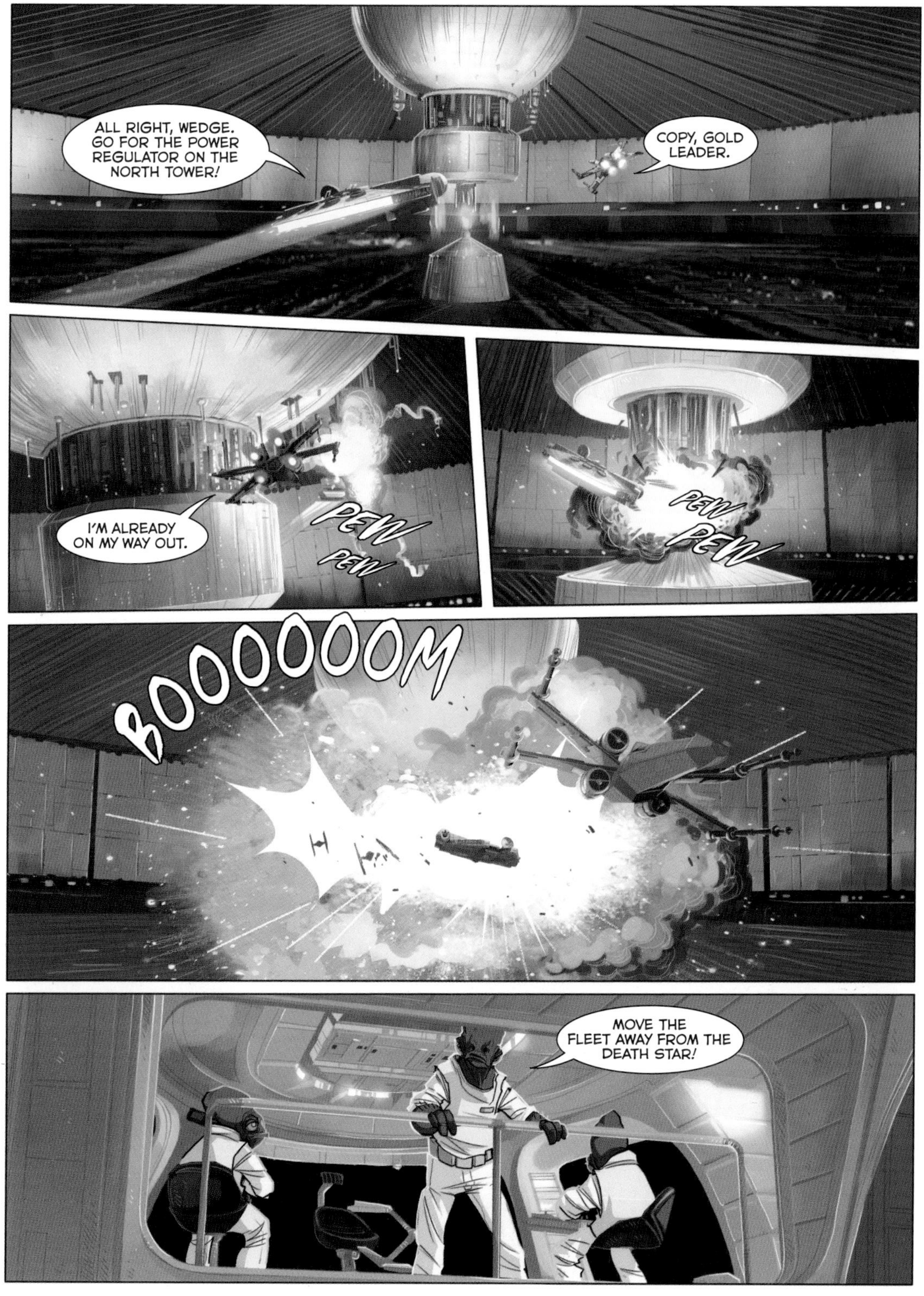
ALL RIGHT, WEDGE. GO FOR THE POWER REGULATOR ON THE NORTH TOWER!
COPY, GOLD LEADER.
I'M ALREADY ON MY WAY OUT.
PEW
PEW
PEW
PEW
BOOOOOOM
MOVE THE FLEET AWAY FROM THE DEATH STAR!

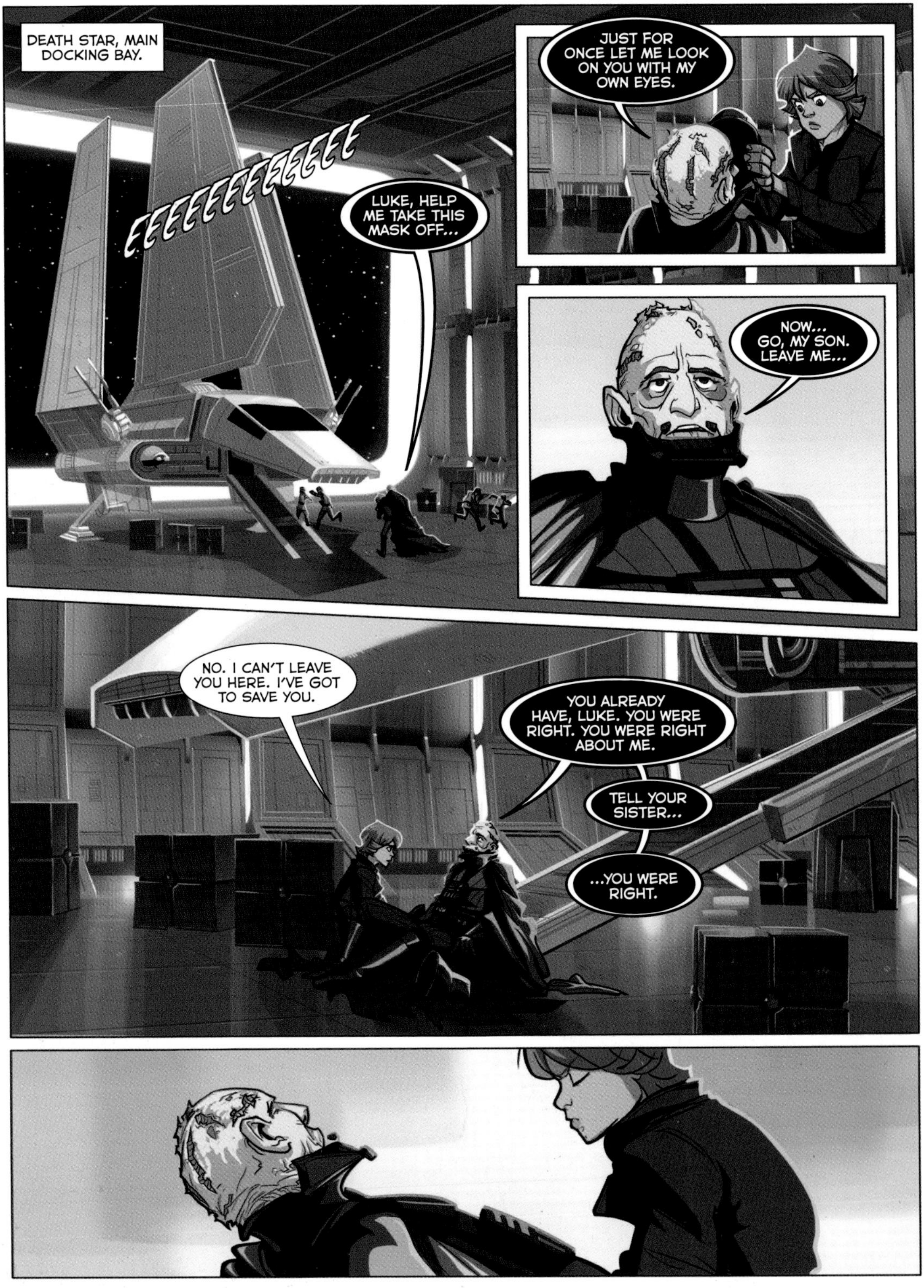
DEATH STAR, MAIN DOCKING BAY.
EEEEEEEEEEEEEE
LUKE, HELP ME TAKE THIS MASK OFF...
JUST FOR ONCE LET ME LOOK ON YOU WITH MY OWN EYES.
NOW... GO, MY SON. LEAVE ME...
NO. I CAN'T LEAVE YOU HERE. I'VE GOT TO SAVE YOU.
YOU ALREADY HAVE, LUKE. YOU WERE RIGHT. YOU WERE RIGHT ABOUT ME.
TELL YOUR SISTER...
...YOU WERE RIGHT.

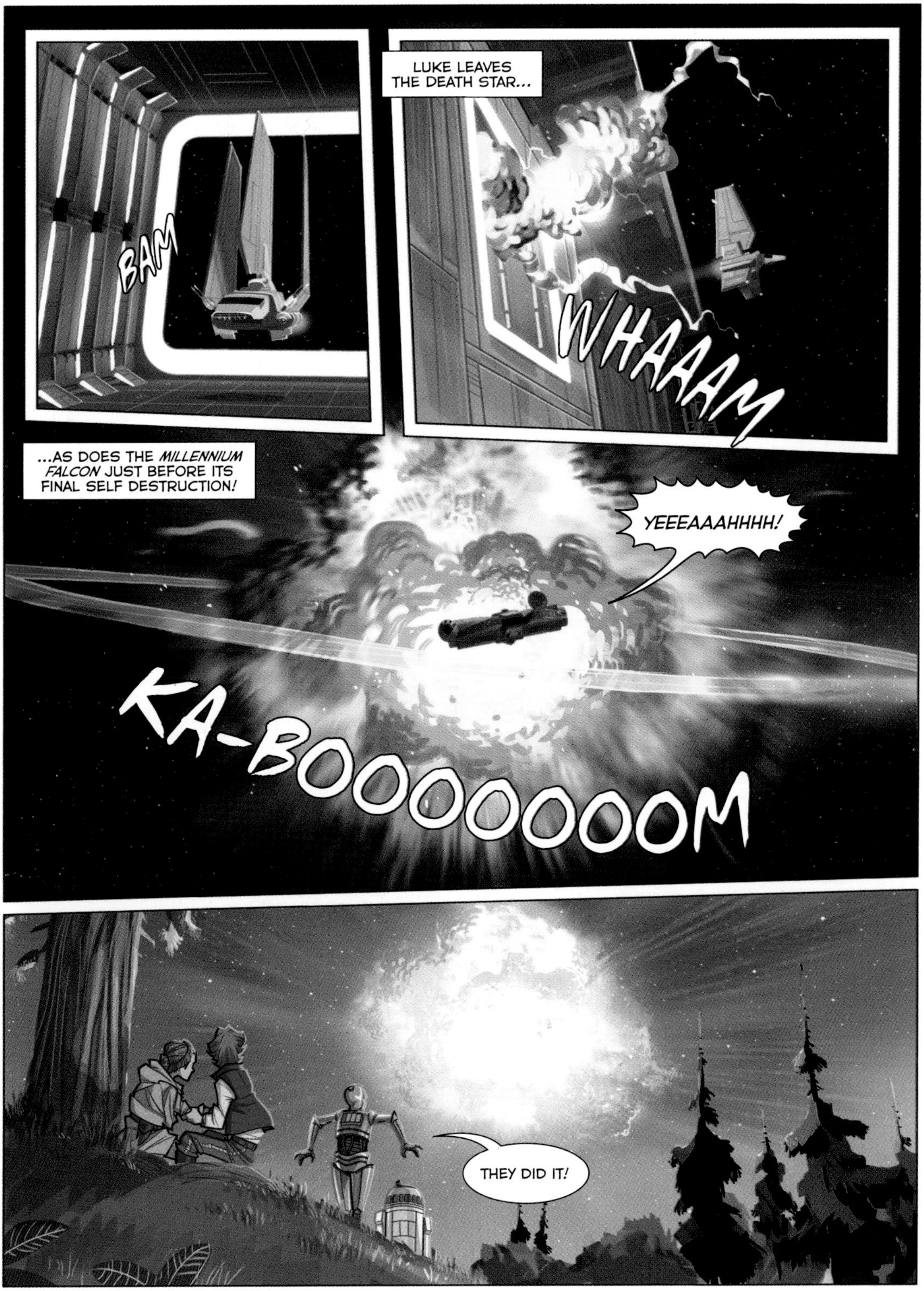
BAM
LUKE LEAVES THE DEATH STAR...
WHAAAM
...AS DOES THE *MILLENNIUM FALCON* JUST BEFORE ITS FINAL SELF DESTRUCTION!
YEEEAAAHHHH!
KA-BOOOOOOOM
THEY DID IT!

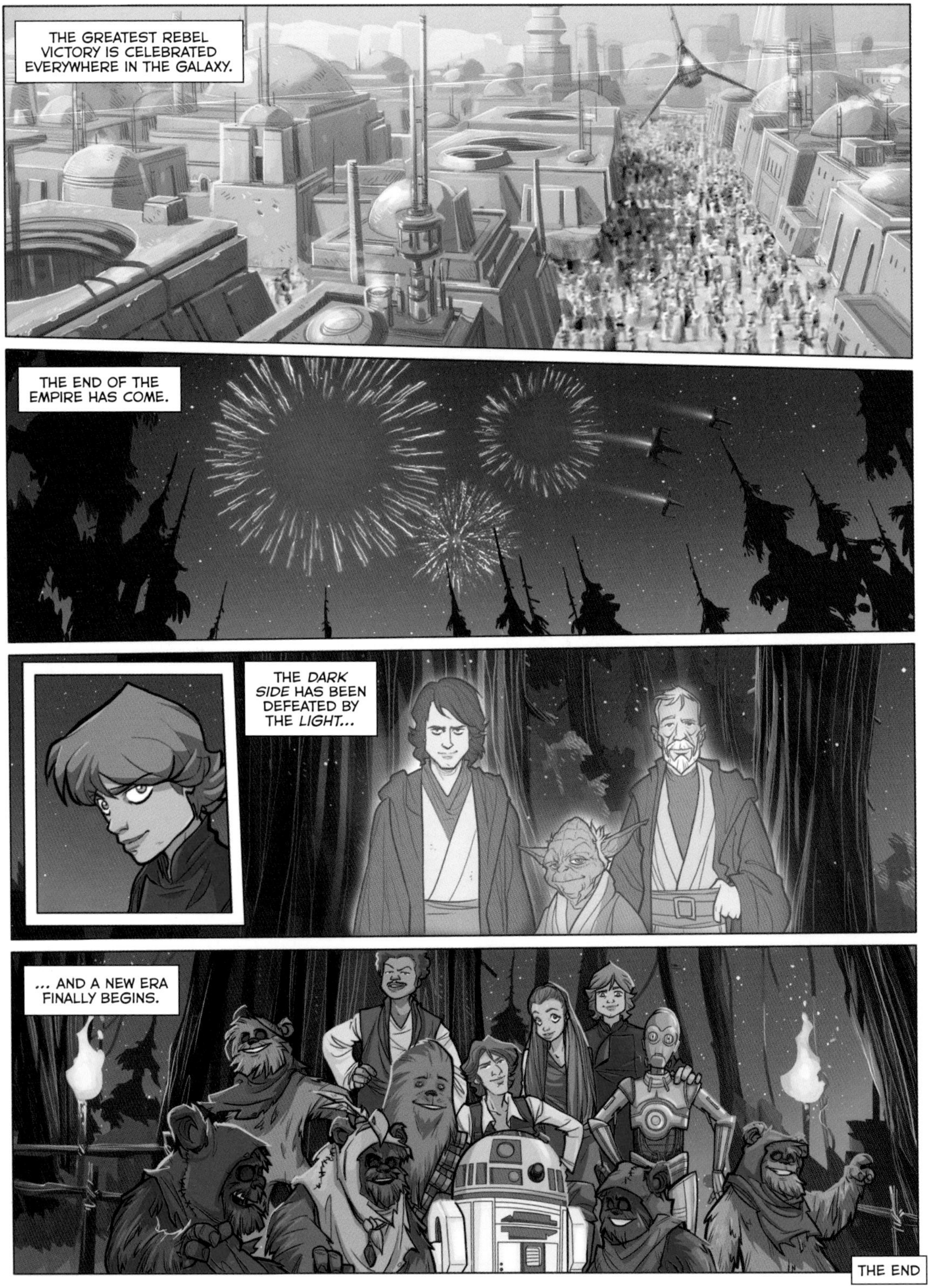
THE GREATEST REBEL VICTORY IS CELEBRATED EVERYWHERE IN THE GALAXY.
THE END OF THE EMPIRE HAS COME.
THE *DARK SIDE* HAS BEEN DEFEATED BY THE *LIGHT*...
... AND A NEW ERA FINALLY BEGINS.
THE END

"YOUR THOUGHTS BETRAY YOU, FATHER. I FEEL THE GOOD IN YOU, THE CONFLICT."

Luke Skywalker

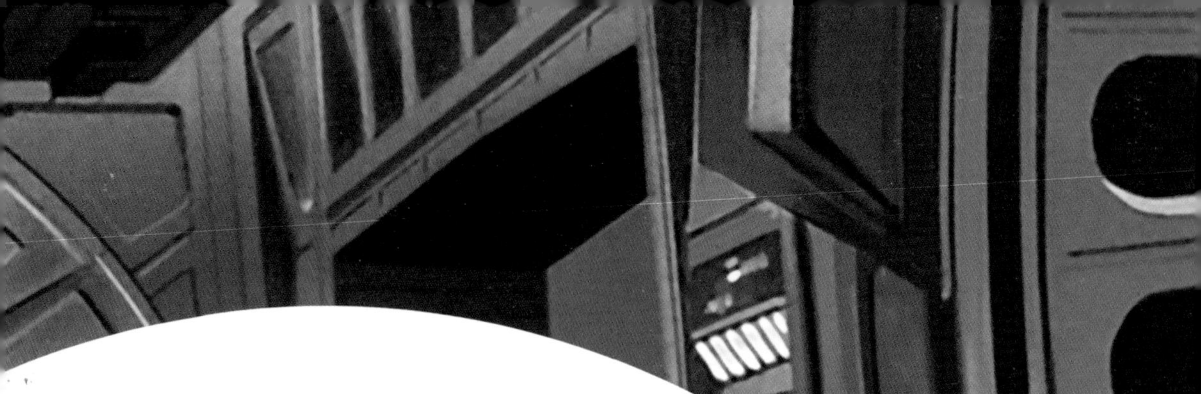

CREDITS

Manuscript Adaptation
Alessandro Ferrari
Character Studies
Igor Chimisso
Layout
Matteo Piana
Clean Up and Ink
Igor Chimisso
Paint (background and settings)
Davide Turotti
Paint (characters)
Kawaii Creative Studio
Cover
Cryssy Cheung
Special Thanks to
Michael Siglain, Jennifer Heddle, Rayne Roberts, Pablo Hidalgo, Leland Chee

Based on the story by George Lucas

DISNEY PUBLISHING WORLDWIDE
Global Magazines, Comics and Partworks

Publisher
Lynn Waggoner

Editorial Team
Bianca Coletti *(Director, Magazines)*
Guido Frazzini *(Director, Comics)*
Stefano Ambrosio *(Executive Editor, New IP)*
Carlotta Quattrocolo *(Executive Editor)*
Camilla Vedove *(Senior Manager, Editorial Development)*
Behnoosh Khalili *(Senior Editor)*
Julie Dorris *(Senior Editor)*

Design
Enrico Soave *(Senior Designer)*
Art
Ken Shue *(VP, Global Art)*
Roberto Santillo *(Creative Director)*
Marco Ghiglione *(Creative Manager)*
Manny Mederos *(Senior Illustration Manager)*
Stefano Attardi *(Illustration Manager)*
Portfolio Management
Olivia Ciancarelli *(Director)*
Business & Marketing
Mariantonietta Galla *(Senior Manager, Franchise)*
Virpi Korhonen *(Editorial Manager)*

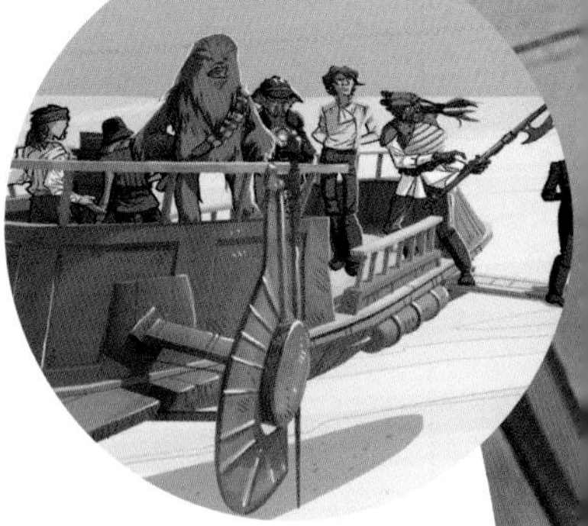

Editing - Graphic Design
Absink, Edizioni BD
Contributors
Carlo Resca

For IDW:
Editors
Justin Eisinger and Alonzo Simon
Collection Design
Christa Miesner

For international rights, contact licensing@idwpublishing.com
ISBN: 978-1-68405-528-9 22 21 20 19 1 2 3 4

Chris Ryall, President & Publisher/CCO • **John Barber**, Editor-in-Chief • **Cara Morrison**, Chief Financial Officer • **Matthew Ruzicka**, Chief Accounting Officer • **David Hedgecock**, Associate Publisher • **Jerry Bennington**, VP of New Product Development • **Lorelei Bunjes**, VP of Digital Services • **Justin Eisinger**, Editorial Director, Graphic Novels and Collections • **Eric Moss**, Sr. Director, Licensing & Business Development

Ted Adams and Robbie Robbins, IDW Founders

www.IDWPUBLISHING.com

Facebook: **facebook.com/idwpublishing** • Twitter: **@idwpublishing** • YouTube: **youtube.com/idwpublishing**
Tumblr: **tumblr.idwpublishing.com** • Instagram: **instagram.com/idwpublishing**

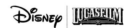